Mistletoe

DAISY JAMES

Mistletoe & Mystery

CANELO

First published in the United Kingdom in 2018 by Canelo

This edition published in the United Kingdom in 2019 by

Canelo Digital Publishing Limited
57 Shepherds Lane
Beaconsfield, Bucks HP9 2DU
United Kingdom

A CIP catalogue record for this book is available from the British Library.

Print ISBN 978 1 78863 571 4
Ebook ISBN 978 1 78863 020 7

Look for more great books at www.canelo.co

Printed and bound in Great Britain by Clays Ltd, Elcograf S.p.A.

To all my family and friends
who make Christmas so special.

Chapter One

"Oh my God! Millie, I'm so jealous! Are you sure Claudia doesn't need a fabulously talented assistant for the Festive Feast course? I could help with the reindeer cupcakes, or the gingerbread Santas, or the St Clements mince pies! And you know how much everyone loves my melt-in-your mouth shortcrust pastry!"

Millie had to smile at Poppy's enthusiasm. She really did wish she could take her friend and fellow pastry chef along with her to Claudia Croft's famous cookery school in the Cotswolds.

"In fact, scratch that. I'd even be prepared to grab my Marigolds and get stuck into the washing up if it meant I could spend the next week in Berryford watching Claudia show a bunch of enthusiast foodies how to rustle up a celebrity-grade Christmas feast. You are sooo lucky! Oh, and not to mention the fact that you'll be able to reacquaint yourself with that hunky estate manager you've never stopped talking about since you came back from St Lucia, the delicious Mr Zach Barker."

Millie felt the heat whoosh into her cheeks and groaned. She had been back from her trip to the Paradise Cookery School in the Caribbean for over two months, but she hadn't been able to hide her feelings for Zach from Poppy who had dug relentlessly for every scrap of detail like an overzealous gossip columnist. Nevertheless, she still wanted to make light of their imminent reunion, despite the eager anticipation that was bubbling in her stomach.

"Poppy, I'm going to Stonelea Manor to co-present the Festive Feast cookery course, not to demonstrate how to manage a country estate. I'll probably be so busy with the tutorials that our paths won't even cross."

"Who are you kidding? I've seen the photos of Zach on your Facebook page – he's *absolutely gorgeous*. If I was in your dainty sequinned sandals, I'd definitely be planning a few unscheduled visits to that cute little stone lodge he calls home, armed with a basket full of freshly baked cinnamon cookies and a bottle of home-made rum punch. Did I tell you how envious I am?"

"You might have mentioned it once or twice!" Millie giggled and rolled her eyes at Poppy as they finished wiping down the marble countertops in

Étienne's, the tiny patisserie in Hammersmith where they were both fortunate enough to work.

Millie adored the atmosphere in the little café; cosy, welcoming, friendly but with a touch of Parisian elegance and the ambient fragrance of warm buttery croissants. However, for her, the best part of the shop was its bay window, hung with a necklace of red, white and blue bunting and showcasing a smorgasbord of delicious delights more akin to a high-end jewellery store – and displaying a wider variety of colours. She loved the neat rows of multicoloured macarons, of pistachio and kiwi mille-feuille, of angel wings and miniature rum babas. Every morning, she would feast her eyes on the display and declare it to be a piece of culinary art, far better than its cousins in the Tate because Étienne's patrons could *taste* their creations!

"Okay, looks like we're done for the day," said Poppy, flicking off the lights and grabbing her duffle bag. "I've got a bottle of chocolate vodka upstairs just crying out to be tested. Come on, let's go and celebrate your good fortune properly."

"My flat or yours?"

"I don't want you to take this personally, Millie, but mine – definitely. I like a bit of seasonal cheer just as much as the next person, but your living room looks like a Christmas volcano has erupted and spewed forth every decoration imaginable! Where on earth did you get all that stuff? I mean, a set of dancing pineapples in sunglasses and Santa suits?"

Millie laughed. "Got those in St Lucia – I love them! I really wanted to buy the matching set of bananas dressed as elves, but I just couldn't cram another thing in my suitcase. Maybe I should give Ella a call and ask her to ship them over for me?"

"I'm no interior decorator but take my advice and try to resist that temptation!"

Millie saw Poppy grin as she opened the door of her apartment nestled in the eaves above the patisserie and just across the hallway from Millie's own tiny studio. Poppy's flat was exactly the same size as hers, but that was where the similarities ended. The décor here reflected her friend's personality to a tee – brash, bohemian, with jewel-bedecked mirrors and lamps that Poppy had designed herself at her Wednesday night art class, a hobby chosen because it meant she could drool over the tutor – a moody French sculptor called François.

Millie sighed and collapsed down on Poppy's over-stuffed orange sofa with a surge of relief. It was the second week in December, the pre-Christmas frenzy had started in earnest, and her feet throbbed their objection to the onslaught of activity. She was already beginning to regret accepting Poppy's invitation instead of heading straight for a long soak in a hot bath filled with her favourite Molton Brown bubbles that her sister Jen had given her for her birthday.

However, when Poppy dropped down on the seat next to her with the promised bottle of vodka and two glasses, she quickly changed her mind about the bath. She accepted a generous measure and sat back against the scarlet silk cushions, curling her legs under her bottom and taking a tentative sip of the popular liquid remedy for the weary.

"Mmm, delicious, thanks Poppy."

"So, what did your mum say when you told her you weren't going over to France for the holidays this year? Did she freak out?"

"Not when I explained why. I mean, it really is a dream come true, isn't it? Mum knows how much I loved presenting the Paradise Cookery School's Chocolate & Confetti course at Claudia's villa in St Lucia. It was a fabulous experience and I learned so much from Ella about Caribbean cooking, but now I've got this amazing chance to work with Claudia Croft herself! Poppy, I've decided that's what I want to do – present cookery classes to enthusiastic food lovers. Sooo… in the new year I'm going to start looking for a new position where I can do just that."

"And leave Étienne's?" Poppy looked scandalised, but her chestnut brown eyes were gentle and understanding. "Only joking. Millie, you could smash whatever you put your mind to. And you've no idea how happy I am to hear you say that. It's about time you moved on to new adventures – you've got a Michelin star, for God's sake. I don't know why you insist on hiding that fact."

"I'm not hiding it."

"Well, you're definitely not shouting about it from the rooftops like I would be!"

Millie watched her friend remove her sparkly hairclips and allow her hair to frame her cheeks in glossy mahogany waves. A whiff of jasmine perfume invaded the air and her heart gave a nip of gratitude for her good fortunate at having someone like Poppy in her life – she really had provided the balm to her ragged soul when she'd arrived in London having been ditched at her own engagement party.

"Actually, all that feels like ancient history now, an episode from someone else's life – someone I don't recognise."

A splash of sadness swished into her chest, but she doused it in a flash. She rarely thought of her ex-fiancé nowadays, and when she did it was with only fleeting regret, not the long, slow burn of agony that had stalked her endlessly until a couple of months ago.

The way Luke had chosen to terminate their two-year relationship had hurt tremendously, but the icing on the pain-filled cupcake had been the discovery that the person he had abandoned her for was her best friend's mother. That morsel of information had been just too much to bear so she had walked out of the restaurant they co-owned, grabbed her suitcase, and ran away to start a new life of anonymity in the metropolis. Poppy had been the first non-family member she had confessed her heartbreak to and her friend had welcomed her into her world with open arms, a cheerful smile, and a surfeit of vodka in a myriad of flavours which had helped to dull the pain.

However, she was happy to report that she was done with licking her wounds. Her confidence in her culinary creativity had returned, and she was ready to launch herself into a new challenge, professional and personal. Her lips twitched at the corners when a fully formed image of the person she had to thank for her renaissance into a normal human being again appeared in her mind's eye: Zach Barker, Claudia's estate manager, whom she'd encountered at the Paradise Cookery School back in September.

Poppy was right. Zach *was* gorgeous; handsome, athletic, inquisitive, with a sharp line in sarcasm and a quirky sense of humour. Even the fact that they occupied opposite ends of the orderliness spectrum hadn't prevented them from connecting on a deeper level than she had expected. She smiled at the memory of the warm, lingering kisses they had shared beneath the swaying palm trees, with the tropical backdrop of the white beaches, sparkling blue ocean and verdant lushness of the vegetation making the whole experience seem so much more romantic.

"So, did Tim tell you why Claudia needs a co-presenter on the Festive Feast course this year? I thought she usually insists on doing all the demonstrations at her cookery school herself? After all, isn't that why most people book the courses – to rub shoulders with a celebrity? Have they accidentally overbooked or something?"

"No, there's only the usual eight fanatical food lovers booked on the course, but Tim said he'd persuaded Claudia to ask for help this year. He's worried about her. Ever since her riding accident she's been complaining about being tired all the time and Tim thinks she needs to build her strength back up after having her leg immobilised in a plaster cast for six weeks."

"And, of course, because of the fantastic job you did at the Paradise Cookery School, Claudia thought of you straight away!"

"Maybe. Anyway, he wants her to take it easy for a while - it's the perfect time over the Christmas holidays - and he plans on taking her over to the Caribbean in the new year for a blast of sunshine. He actually wanted Claudia to cancel the Festive Feast course, but she refused because she didn't want to let the students down."

"Claudia's an amazing woman," sighed Poppy, shoving a handful of home-made toffee-and-pecan popcorn into her mouth and selecting a lock of hair to twist around her fingers. "I've got all her cookery books. Hey, if I give you a couple, do you think you could ask her to sign them for me?"

"Sure," Millie laughed, draining her glass and running the tip of her tongue along her lower lip to savour every last drop. "You know, I'm really looking forward to meeting Claudia face-to-face, but I don't mind admitting that I'm also a little bit nervous. I mean, co-presenting a course with the doyenne of desserts! What if I mess up? What if…" Millie's eyes widened as she tucked an escaped curl behind her ear. "What if I smash a priceless vase or drop a bottle of vintage Krug? You know what I'm like, Poppy. Mishap Millie is what Zach calls me, and he's spot on!"

"And we've been working on those issues since you got back from the Caribbean and you're doing great," Poppy assured Millie loyally, handing her the bowl of popcorn that complimented the chocolate vodka perfectly.

"Not great! Remember yesterday when I dribbled a generous helping of crème Anglaise on the sleeve of that customer's brand-new Paul Smith sweater? It was only Étienne's swift intervention with an offer of afternoon-tea-for-two on the house that stopped him from sending over his dry-cleaning bill."

Poppy laughed as she leaned forward to refill their glasses.

"Look, Millie, you are an awesome chef. Your culinary creations will speak louder than your haphazard methods. Just use the week to learn everything you can from Claudia and when you get back you'll walk into that coveted presenting job."

"Maybe." Millie paused as something else occurred to her. "You know, Tim said something else that worried me."

"What did he say?"

"That one of the reasons Claudia didn't want to cancel the Festive Feast course this year was because it was going to be the last one."

"So that's weird. Why would Claudia want to stop running the courses?"

"I asked Tim that very question. He said it was complicated and that Claudia would explain everything when I got there, but that she's devastated. It could be one of the reasons why she's been feeling under the weather recently and has agreed to get additional help this year."

"Well, maybe you could offer your services every year from now on? Did I tell you how envious I am? Are my cheeks turning fifty shades of green? Oh, I bet Berryford is so romantic at this time of year – everything twinkling with fairy lights, the aroma of cinnamon and cloves floating through the crisp winter air, and the whole scene set to the sound-track of White Christmas. Id–dyl–lic. Wouldn't it be amazing if it actually *does* snow?"

"No way! You know how much I hate the snow."

"Oh, but it would be the icing on the Christmas cake. A cute Cotswolds village wrapped in a soft blanket of white. A chance to sit around a blazing log fire, hugging cups of warm mulled wine, sharing bodily warmth with the local heartthrob and kissing underneath the mistletoe. Hey, Millie, maybe you should carry an emergency spring of mistletoe in your back pocket so you can whip it out when Zach's least expecting it. How can he refuse? It's tradition. Isn't that what Christmas is all about? Tradition?" asked Poppy, her dark eyes sparkling as she wallowed in her own personal version of Yuletide heaven.

Millie had to agree. Apart from the higher than average risk of snow, she adored everything about

Christmas. It was the perfect excuse to fill every nook and cranny with as much festive paraphernalia as possible; tinsel, baubles, snow globes, bunting, fairy lights – her flat was stuffed to the rafters with so many decorations it looked like a hyperactive elf's grotto – and she loved it! Who would choose the stark, clean lines of Scandinavian minimalism when you could hang a hand-embroidered snowman above the fireplace and house a whole herd of flashing reindeers on the front lawn?

Yes, she was a complete Christmas fanatic, always had been, and so was her sister Jen, much to their mother's disgust. Monique had embraced her French heritage and insisted on dressing her converted barn high in the hills of Provence with a simple fir tree and nothing else, preferring to splash her cash on all the foodie treats associated with the season - cinnamon palmiers, bûche de Noël, and a spectacular caramel croquembouche centrepiece - rather than the decorations and excessive gift-giving Millie and Jen loved so much. Millie knew she was going to *love* her week's sojourn at Stonelea Manor whipping up a long list of traditional recipes for a bunch of busy professionals.

"I wish you were coming to Berryford, Poppy. I'm not sure what Tim meant about it being the last course, but Stonelea Manor is their home, so perhaps Claudia just wants to move the school to different premises, or to concentrate all her efforts on getting the Caribbean branch properly established. I know she has plans to reinvigorate the cocoa plantation so she can make her own chocolate and offer tours of the estate to the students. That's bound to take up a lot of her time and energy."

"All the more reason for you to offer your services in the Cotswolds. And you know what the best thing about that is?"

"What?"

"You'll get to spend some real quality time with the most handsome estate manager this side of the Atlantic! It'll be the ideal opportunity to find out if the spark you both felt in the Caribbean paradise has transferred to the 'paradise' of the English countryside. If so, then you could be on to something magical."

Despite their busy lives in different parts of the country - hers in London, Zach's in the Cotswolds now that he'd returned from St Lucia - they had stayed in touch via email and the occasional text. She was excited about seeing him again, or she had been until earlier that afternoon when she'd read Zach's response to the news of her imminent arrival; a concise text stating that they had 'a lot to talk about' when she got to Berryford - and she had no idea what that meant. Could she have misread the signals? Just in case she had, she intended to play down the fizz of anticipation bubbling through her veins.

"I'm not sure things would work between me and Zach. We *are* very different."

"Haven't you heard of the expression 'opposites attract'? And have you forgotten that cocktail-infused confession you made last Saturday night about how alive you felt whenever you were in Zach's company? But, in the event that nothing happens between the two of you – there's always the Mistletoe Ball on Christmas Eve for you to look forward to."

Millie noticed a glint of mischief in Poppy's eyes, a sure sign for her to be on her guard.

"And?"

"What do you mean?" said Poppy, all innocence.

"Poppy, I know you're cooking something up."

"Well, a little French birdie told me that François and his brother Phillipe will be there, and I might just have happened to mention that I have a gorgeous single friend with a halo of sunshine-coloured curls who's a whizz at knocking up a kaleidoscope of macarons, and who also just happens to be half-French too."

"Poppy! I can organise my own love life, thank you very much."

"Clearly not, as you haven't had a date since you got back from St Lucia two months ago. I know you profess to be over Luke, but the only way to prove it is to start dating with a vengeance. Open your heart to the possibility that there is someone amazing out there waiting to make you happy! And what better time to start than Christmas? All you have to do is trust your friendly neighbourhood Cupid and agree to a double-date with a certain chocolate-eyed Frenchman, with skin the colour of liquid caramel and a penchant for dousing himself in an excessive amount of spicy cologne."

"Poppy…"

"Look, Millie, just go to the Cotswolds, have fun at Claudia's cookery school, and if nothing happens with Zach, you can zoom back here on Christmas Eve ready to enjoy the festive season sprinkled with a little Parisian *amour!*"

Chapter Two

With the tinkle of *Frosty the Snowman* still ringing in her ears from the cab ride, Millie made her way across the concourse of Paddington Station. A curl of excitement, mingled with a generous dose of trepidation, wriggled through her chest as she contemplated what the week ahead would hold. Could she really be about to present a cookery course to eight enthusiastic foodies in the presence of the celebrity cookery book writer, Claudia Croft – in the kitchen of her fabulous manor house in the Cotswolds?

The previous night, she and Poppy had googled Stonelea Manor in Berryford and had been astonished at its picturesque splendour. Set against a Turneresque backdrop of rolling lawns and thick woodland, the Grade II listed building looked as if it had been dusted in a generous pinch of cinnamon. However, it wasn't its architectural magnificence that had caused Millie to pause and drool, but the photographs of the kitchen. She recognised it immediately from Claudia's cookery books and couldn't believe that on Monday morning she would be standing behind the marble-topped workstation issuing instructions on how to craft the perfect meringue.

A sudden blast of arctic air walloped her in the face, whipping the breath from her lips and bringing her back to the present. Goose pimples rippled over every inch of her skin and her teeth chattered uncontrollably. Much worse were the curious glances she was attracting from her fellow travellers at the ridiculous attire she had chosen to wear to brave a British winter.

She dragged the sides of her flimsy cotton cardigan around her chest, cursing the fact that she had left all her winter clothes at her sister's after the emergency evacuation from Luke's flat in April and hadn't had time to retrieve them. However, as she lived two storeys above the place where she worked, a down-filled jacket had not been high on her list of essentials, especially when there was such limited storage space. Her thoughts scooted back to her sojourn at Claudia's villa in St Lucia where she had been fortunate enough to spend some time lounging by the pool in a bikini, sipping strawberry margaritas to a backing track of reggae rhythms rippling through the sun-drenched air. Paradise! She had always been a sun worshipper – a fact she put down to being a July baby – which was the reason she had planned to spend the Christmas holidays with her mum in Provence, even if it had meant she would have to partner her at her weekly Salsa classes.

However, the wintery temperature was a small price to pay for the opportunity to spend quality time with an accomplished chef, so Millie grabbed the handle of her wheelie suitcase and stalked towards the flashing Departures board, relieved to see that her train to Berryford was already waiting at platform three. She hitched her canvas bag higher up her shoulder, surreptitiously tapping the contents to make sure her trusty scrap box of recipes that went everywhere with her was safely stowed, and went in search of her carriage.

She selected a window seat and slumped into the corner, rubbing her palms on her thighs and blowing on her fingers in an effort to warm up. The train left on time and almost immediately she felt a veil of lethargy descend. Houses flashed by, their dark facades dotted with rectangles of amber light, highlighting the silhouettes of families gathered around the television or computer screen. As the urban sprawl melted into fields, the rhythmic rocking encouraged her to close her eyes for a few seconds, allowing her to savour the solitude of being in transit.

She must have fallen asleep because when she peeled her eyes open and glanced out of the window a bolt of shock crashed into her chest. The scene beyond the glass came directly from a Hollywood producer's demand for a typical English winter backdrop – and boy had those set designers delivered! A soft blanket of white had been tossed over the fields and rolling hills, obliterating the undulations. Huge, feather-like snowflakes fell languidly from the leaden sky, adding another layer to the wintry scene.

A glance at her watch told Millie it was almost three o'clock. Dusk was beginning to tickle the horizon with a crimson-purple hue, and the whole vista looked Christmas-card perfect, especially when a lone church spire punctured the swathe of snow reminding her of childhood Christmases when her father was still around. However, it was one thing to appreciate the scenic charm of the landscape from the comfort and warmth of a train seat, quite another to have to actually set foot in the loathsome white stuff.

A shiver cascaded down her spine as she did a mental inventory of the clothes she had stuffed into her suitcase. Feeling she should make an effort to look the part when standing at Claudia's side, she had packed her favourite Hobbs tops and a lovely crimson silk dress she planned to debut at the celebration party on the last day of the week-long course. Even if she wore every last stitch, she'd still freeze to death on her trek from the train station to the car Claudia had said she was sending to collect her. Her heart sank to her toes as the train pressed further into Oxfordshire and the gentle drift of snowflakes morphed into a blizzard. Visibility from the already opaque train window was nil.

At the nearest station to Berryford, an obliging commuter helped her to lift her luggage down from the train to the platform and she smarted at the amusement in his eyes.

"I'd put a coat on if I were you, love."

Millie glared at him for stating the obvious before bestowing him with one of the typically Gallic shrugs she and her sister Jen had inherited from their mother. Unlike Jen, who had embraced all things English when their family had relocated to her father's home town from Lourmarin, Millie still struggled with the resurgence of her French roots whenever she was stressed, angry or had overindulged on Prosecco. She had no problem whatsoever with that; she loved the trace of French in her accent that reminded her of the sunshine-filled childhood she had enjoyed in the south of France, where the necessity of owning a winter coat was non-existent.

She made her way towards the waiting room, dragging her wheelie suitcase in her wake, and lunged through the door, where, to her delight and tear-inducing relief, the central heating was on full blast.

She slumped down into a seat to recover her breath and for the first time wished Claudia had decided to run her Festive Feast cookery course in her St Lucian villa high up in the hills above Soufrière, overlooking the spectacular sight of the twin Pitons, the emerald pyramids of rock poking out of the Caribbean Sea like the spines of a sleeping dinosaur.

She sprung the lock on her suitcase and grabbed another cardigan, shivering like a baby kitten and cursing her lack of forward planning. A few seconds later, her vivid stream of weather-themed invectives was interrupted by a buzz from her pocket and she fumbled with frozen fingers to answer her call.

"Hey, it's Maddening Millie! Welcome to Gloucestershire! Where are you?"

Millie rolled her eyes, but the sound of Zach's voice was like nectar to her ears. "I'm sitting in the waiting room trying to get some feeling back into my hands."

"Stay there. I'll come and get you."

A splurge of warmth that had nothing to do with the ambient temperature spread through Millie's chest as she replayed an image of Zach in his figure-hugging black tee-shirt and denim shorts as they explored the exotic sights of St Lucia together. Despite her denials to Poppy, she couldn't ignore the fact that a large part of the attraction of spending the week in

Berryford was so that she would be able to spend time with Zach again. Just being in his presence made her nerve endings zing, yet she struggled to describe the relationship niche into which they had fallen. Was it friendship, companionship or something altogether more complicated? She was leaning more towards the third option and maybe spending this week together in more mundane surroundings would help her to figure it out.

A flurry of snowflakes danced in the air as an elderly couple stumbled through the waiting room door, clad in sensible fleeces, waterproof cagoules and robust walking boots with thick woollen socks turned over at the ankle. They glanced in her direction, ready to exchange a cheery seasonal greeting before performing a comedic double-take at her unsuitable attire. She gifted them a confident smile and they quickly averted their eyes.

Who in their right mind would willingly come to a place like this in the middle of a snowstorm the last week before Christmas? Millie wondered. Wasn't there an over-heated cathedral of consumerism to meander through in search of that perfect gift for Aunt Marge? In fact, if she had known she would be battling through a snow-filled Armageddon, she too might have thought twice about accepting Claudia's offer.

Within minutes, the door burst open again and her heart performed a flipflop of pleasure at the sight in front of her. Even with a woolly hat pulled down over his ears and a stylish Dr Who-style scarf wound artfully around the collar of his black denim jacket, Zach Barker was eye-poppingly handsome and her body's instant reaction to his arrival told her everything she needed to know.

Unfortunately, from the look on his face, he was clearly not thinking the same. Millie watched him run his eyes over her skimpy attire and saw his lips twitch into that familiar smirk, causing the cute dimples to appear like brackets in his cheeks, and his dark eyes to sparkle with mischief.

"I see you have come prepared for a day out at the beach instead of a journey through the snowbound countryside? What's the matter? Didn't anyone tell you it was December? Is that your luggage?"

"Yes."

"Where's your coat?"

Zach's eyes rested on her sequinned Converse trainers for a few beats before flicking back up to her face, his jaw loose with incredulity. His expression couldn't have been more amazed if she was stood before him naked.

"Erm, I didn't bring a coat. It wasn't snowing when I left London, and anyway, I plan on spending most of my time in the hi-tech *centrally-heated* kitchen of Stonelea Manor," retorted Millie, aware of the defensive note that had crept into her voice, a familiar occurrence when speaking to super-sensible Zach. "I'll be fine. Just point me in the direction of your car and I'll make a run for it."

"You've got to be joking? It's minus two out there! Here, take my jacket and channel your inner Usain Bolt. Come on!"

And before she could refuse, Zach had handed her his coat, grabbed the handle of her suitcase and jogged from the waiting room towards the car park. She rushed in his wake, slotting her arms into his still-warm jacket, revelling in the familiar fragrance of his cologne that lingered on the fabric.

When they reached Zach's car, the meteorological Gods decided to go for broke and fling everything in their armoury at them. With snowflakes lashing angrily at the windscreen like an icy carwash, Millie heaved a sigh of relief when she slammed the door and leaned her head back against the headrest.

"Urgh! I hate the snow!"

"Now why doesn't that surprise me? Don't you think it has a certain aesthetic beauty? Erasing all the sharp edges and angular gables of the ugly architecture to produce a minimalist simplicity? Oh, no, sorry I forgot, I'm talking to Amelia Harper, the Queen of

Clutter and Chaos!" chuckled Zach as he struggled to steer the vehicle deeper into the countryside through the ever-increasing snow drifts.

Millie had grown accustomed to Zach's unique line in playful banter and chose not to rise to the bait. Anyway, she could see from the twinkle in his eyes and the turn of his lips that he was happy to see her.

"How far is it to Berryford?"

In reply, Zach took a sharp right-hand turn and came to an abrupt halt outside an attractive stone lodge next to a pair of magnificent carved pillars that Millie recognised from her google search as the entrance to Stonelea Manor. Visibility had improved just enough for her to get a glimpse through the windscreen of the handsome house nestled amidst a cotton wool wonderland. It was as though the property had been transported from the pages of a fairy tale and was even more beautiful than the photographs on the internet had indicated.

Apart from the honeyed stone and matching rooftiles, the building presented a pleasing symmetry, with dual mullioned windows on either side of the grand front entrance, all set against a backdrop of quite sinister woodland, a living labyrinth that could conceal a myriad of dangers. A necklace of wrought-iron lampposts meandered from the entrance gate to the front steps, but it was impossible to ascertain the precise route of the driveway.

"Why have we stopped here?" she asked, trying to ignore the squirm of apprehension agitating at her chest.

"Because, as you can see, the snow is over a foot deep and there's no way this battered old Golf will make it to the manor."

"So how are you proposing we get there?"

"We need to transfer to a more appropriate means of transport. Forward planning – ever heard of it?" Zach teased as he swung his legs out of the driver's seat and jogged around the back of the vehicle to open the boot, calling through to where Millie was still clinging to the warmth of the passenger seat. "However, even I hadn't anticipated that you'd turn up dressed for a tropical cocktail party in the Caribbean."

"I'm not dressed for..."

"Here, you'd better put these on," said Zach, tossing a jumble of cloth into her arms.

Millie scrunched up her nose in revulsion as a whiff of dead ferret, mingled with a soupçon of ammonia, invaded her nostrils.

"I'm not wearing these!"

"You will if you don't want to die of hyper-thermia."

"I think I'll risk it!" she snapped, as she unfolded the garment to reveal an ancient brown wax jacket with a dung-coloured fleece hand-sewn into the lining. It was so long the hem would probably skim her ankles.

"It wasn't a request, Millie. Put it on. The sooner we get down to the manor the better."

She reconsidered her initial diagnosis of the origins of the pungent aroma. The smell wasn't ammonia – it was linseed oil interspersed with horse manure and something else a little earthier. A hint of nausea scratched at the back of her throat.

"The hat and gloves are in the pockets."

"Is this a wind-up? Because if it is, I don't think it's very funny."

Knowing Zach's quirky sense of humour and the mischievous way he had coaxed her to experience new and exhilarating experiences in the past, Millie wouldn't have put it past him to whip out a camera as soon as she stood before him in the stupid get-up and to upload the image to his Facebook page. She scrutinised his face, a face that had frequented her dreams more often than she cared to admit, and watched him remove his hat and run his fingers through his spiky black hair then scratch at his unshaven chin; a sure sign of anxiety.

"It's not a wind-up, Millie. We've got to go - now. The weather guys are predicting one of the most severe snow storms for ten years and they're warning against all non-essential travel. We're lucky to have got this far."

"But… Oh, okay."

Heaving a sigh, Millie slotted her arms into the coat, huddling into its folds to seek out every scrap of warmth. She completed the sartorial car crash by yanking on the knitted hat and gloves and was surprised when an image of Zach's elegantly attired ex-girlfriend floated into her thoughts. She had met Chloe in St Lucia when she'd turned up unannounced to persuade Zach to rekindle their relationship, but her plan hadn't produced the result she had been hoping for and, much to Millie's relief, she'd spent the rest of her stay in Rodney Bay in the north of the island with her sister.

"Welcome to the Cotswolds, Amelia Harper. It's great to see you again," Zach whispered, leaning forward to tuck Millie's hair into the collar, gifting her with a wide grin and another delicious dash of his lemony aftershave, the soft warmth of his breath on her cheeks sending sparkles of pleasure through her frozen veins. "Come on."

Zach spun on his heels and disappeared around the back of the lodge, dragging her suitcase behind him. She followed at a safe distance, her shoulders hunched, spirals of breath pirouetting through the freezing air in front of her, aware that her lower lip was protruding like a recalcitrant teenager.

The day was well into its final act and long fissures of indigo and scarlet rippled over the horizon. She glanced up at the clouds, the colour of an angry bruise, paused briefly in their eternal cycle while they geared up for a repeat dumping of their frozen contents. Every step she took required a tremendous effort and she estimated that at the rate she was progressing, it would take an hour to get to the manor and that was without factoring in having to haul her suitcase through the snow. A blast of icy rain slapped her face, and, if she hadn't been so completely fed up, she would have laughed. Boy, was it cold!

But where had Zach disappeared to?

A sharp blast of throttle from behind the lodge sent shockwaves through her chest, and as she rounded the corner she was faced with a terrible sight. There was Zach, enveloped in a cloud of exhaust fumes, revving the engine of a canary yellow snowmobile and proffering a matching helmet.

"Hurry up. Jump on."

Her inability to move her extremities had nothing to do with ice clogging up her veins. A swirl of horror tightened the muscles in her stomach as realisation dawned and she gawped at Zach like a traumatised goldfish. Strapped to the back of the machine more regularly used by adrenaline junkies was her wheelie suitcase and the comprehension was complete.

"No way am I getting on the back of that!"

"You don't have any choice if you want to get to Stonelea Manor today. Now stop whinging and hop on. Grab my waist and hold on tight. We've only got about five minutes of daylight left and I don't want to risk driving this thing in the dark."

Zach reversed the angry insect and pulled up beside Millie. She swallowed down on the maelstrom of emotions churning through her body, hoisted up the mammoth coat, and threw her leg over the seat. But Zach pulled away much quicker than she had anticipated, and she tumbled backward from the seat, landing in a conveniently soft pile of snow, legs akimbo. Zach had the audacity to laugh and she scowled at him as she pushed herself upright and dusted down her glamourous wax coat, trying to remember the last time she had felt as wet and miserable as she did at that precise moment, dressed like a gamekeeper's moll and frozen to her core.

"Ah, Millie, I've missed you," Zach chuckled as he shook his head with amusement. "Life definitely has less sparkle without you in it! This time, grab hold tight!"

Millie jumped back onto the throbbing machine and snaked her arms around Zach's waist, leaning her cheek against his back to protect her face from the persistent onslaught of hailstones as they made their way, bucking and bouncing like an arctic kangaroo, to the front steps of the manor. The wind had picked up its velocity to ferocious, whipping up a helix of snow only to dump its frozen treasure on to the road ahead.

Just as Millie's ears began to scream with a searing pain, and she thought she couldn't cling on to Zach a minute longer, he swung to the left and cut the engine. In her eagerness to escape from her undignified transport, Millie kicked her leg high, missed her footing and tumbled to the ground for a second time.

If she didn't know better, she would have suspected Zach had orchestrated the whole scenario. As it was, it was probably the most undignified arrival Stonelea Manor had ever witnessed in its two-hundred-year history and she sent up a prayer to her personal director of fate that Claudia wasn't watching the impromptu farce from one of the upstairs windows.

Chapter Three

"Millie, darling, it's so good to meet you in person at last! Oh, you poor thing, you look frozen! Come in! Come in! I've made some hot chocolate and a fresh batch of chilli-chocolate brownies which should warm you up in no time. Isn't the weather just dreadful?" declared Claudia as she greeted Millie on the threshold of Stonelea Manor with a smile radiating welcome and warmth before enveloping her in a Chanel No 5-infused hug. "Can I tempt you to join us, Zach?"

"No, thanks, Claudia. I'm sure you and Millie have a lot to catch up on, but I'll see you tomorrow night at the Berryford tree-lighting ceremony."

"Okay, but would you mind popping your head round the door of Tim's workshop before you go back to the lodge? He mentioned something about a sprocket, or a socket, or it could have been a rocket! And whilst you're there, maybe you could introduce my husband to a dose of your superb organisational skills? That place is starting to look like a cemetery for rust-blistered tools. In fact, things have got so bad recently I'm worried about him injuring himself! And what if one of our more inquisitive cookery school visitors inadvertently strays from a stroll in the gardens and meets a grizzly end in the jaws of one of those so-called life-enhancing mechanical contraptions he's invented? I really wish he would stick to designing houses instead of dreaming of being the next Thomas Edison."

Claudia rolled her eyes in frustration, but Millie could see the genuine affection in her expression. She also filed away the very welcome knowledge that Tim Croft was a fellow enthusiast when it came to clutter – she suspected they were going to get along just fine.

"Will do," smiled Zach, tightening his scarf as he prepared to brave the elements once more. "Catch you both later."

"Bye, Zach. Thanks for the lift."

"No problem."

"Why don't you leave your suitcase at the bottom of the stairs and come through to the kitchen, Millie?"

Millie followed Claudia into the oak-panelled hallway, smiling at the clickety-clack of her host's heels on the polished parquet flooring. The whole room looked like a 1920s murder mystery film set, complete with a magnificent grandfather clock standing to attention like a soldier on parade. Straight ahead of her stood the most magnificent mahogany staircase, its banister just crying out for a session of unrestrained sliding when no one was watching.

A surprisingly modest fir tree, dressed in twinkling fairy lights and a tasteful selection of red and gold baubles and almost concealed from view by a painted Chinese screen, was the only nod to the fact that it was the Christmas season. Where were the holly wreaths, the pine-cone-and-mistletoe garlands, the tinsel draped over the picture frames? It was another mystery to add to her lengthening list.

"Wow, this entrance hall is amazing!"

"Wait until you see where we'll be delivering the Festive Feast course on Monday! Come on."

A whoosh of heat whipped into Millie's cheeks as she realised she was still wearing the voluminous wax jacket Zach had insisted she put on. Whilst Claudia's back was turned, she quickly shrugged it off and stuffed the offensive-smelling garment underneath an antique console table, causing a Clarice Cliff vase to wobble precariously. All thought of the strange absence of festive decorations vanished from her mind as a pirouette of excitement began to wind through her chest, culminating in a blast of unadulterated pleasure when Claudia pushed open an oak-panelled door to reveal the house's engine room in all its splendour.

Millie couldn't prevent her jaw from gaping as she feasted her eyes on every modern appliance a professional chef could possibly ask for; stainless-steel food mixers, liquidisers, juicers, copper pans of various sizes, and pots filled with every utensil imaginable from balloon whisks to spatulas, slotted spoons to cake slices. Two enormous American-style refrigerators stood sentry at a second door which Millie suspected would lead to an old-fashioned pantry filled with a kaleidoscope of ingredients, more than any self-respecting chef could ever need.

The whole room was a veritable Aladdin's cave for the passionate culinary junkie and she couldn't wait to spend a few hours familiarizing herself with every last corkscrew and cheese grater. However, her eyes were drawn to the central island unit topped with white marble – so familiar from the *Claudia Cooks...* cookery books, but what the glossy photographs hadn't shown were the four identical workstations facing the island unit, decorated in a variety of pastel shades, each with its own sink and swan-necked tap, from where the students watched Claudia demonstrate her recipes before attempting to recreate them for themselves under her expert guidance.

When Millie had finished drooling over the facilities, she switched her attention to the French windows that stretched the full width of the wall to her left forming an orangery-like extension presided over by a twelve-seater white marble table where the amateur cooks could sit down and sample their creations.

"Claudia, it's…"

Millie struggled to choose an adjective sufficient to describe how she was feeling. In that precise moment, her decision to change career direction from working as a pastry chef at Étienne's patisserie to presenting her own cookery courses – even if it was at the local school or college – crystallised. She knew it was time for her to grasp her courage by the scruff of the neck and embark on the next chapter in her culinary story.

"No words necessary, Millie. Your face says it all!" laughed Claudia, the delight evident in her voice. "Now, grab a seat and I'll get you that hot chocolate."

"Thanks, Claudia. I think the feeling in my fingers has just about returned."

Millie sat down on one of the barstools at the island unit and switched her scrutiny from the room she would be spending most of her time in over the next week to the person she would be spending it with. She estimated Claudia's age to be anywhere between thirty-five and forty-five. With flawless skin and mesmerising blue eyes, even relaxing at home on a Saturday evening she looked every inch the celebrated chef in a figure-enhancing dark green dress, emerald earrings the size of olives and one of the jaunty Hermès scarves she was famous for tied elegantly at her neck. Unlike Millie's unruly corkscrew curls, Claudia's caramel-coloured graduated bob was salon fresh, highlighted with golden strands that shone under the intensity of the overhead lighting, and her makeup was photoshoot ready.

"I've popped in a tot of rum for medicinal purposes," smiled Claudia, handing Millie a mug decorated with the Claudia Croft logo and sliding into the seat opposite her. "I knew you'd love this kitchen. Tim designed it for me from scratch; he really listened to my brief and made sure I got exactly what I wanted - and more. He's a talented architect - I just wish he could reign in his obsession with squirreling away every last screw and nail '*in case it comes in useful one day!*' Let me give you a piece of advice, Millie – steer clear of his workshop if you value your sanity, unless, of course, you happen to be a sucker for broken bits of old washing machines, which I doubt."

Millie sipped the sugar-sweet, chocolatey heaven that was in her mug, savouring the way it slipped down her throat like liquid velvet and sent warmth cascading into every extremity. She didn't think now was the right time to confide in Claudia about her own personal battle with the clutter monsters – in her case of the culinary variety. There was plenty of time for her employer to find out about that flaw in her personality during the next seven days. Or perhaps she was doing herself a disservice? Over the last few weeks, with Poppy's encouragement, she *had* been working hard on her predisposition to bring chaos to an empty room.

"Claudia, it's beautiful. You are so lucky to call this wonderful place your home as well as your place of work."

"You're right. I am very fortunate, even more so because you've agreed to step into the breach once again, Millie. I know I've said this already, but I'll be eternally grateful for what you and Ella achieved in St Lucia with the Chocolate & Confetti course – not to mention the tremendous success of Imogen and Alex's wedding celebrations! It really is beyond the call of duty to ask you to come to my aid for a second time. Étienne is an angel for letting you have another week off from the patisserie – although that might have something to do with Tim's offer of our villa for two weeks in January as compensation! He adores the sunshine, not to mention the plentiful supply of rum cocktails. You should ask him to tell you about his exploits when we were studying at Le Cordon Bleu in Paris together."

Claudia ran her fingers through her hair, allowing the glossy tresses to fall back around her cheeks like toffee-coloured angel's wings. She expelled a long sigh of fatigue and for the first time Millie noticed the dark smudges of exhaustion beneath her eyes that no amount of expertly applied foundation had been able to erase.

"Is everything okay, Claudia?" she asked tentatively. "When Tim called me last week he sounded worried about you?"

"I'm fine. I just don't seem to be able to shift this sluggishness that's been grabbing at my bones since I had my riding accident. Some days my legs feel like they're encased in concrete and every step's a struggle. I really don't know why I'm so tired all the time because I sleep like a churchyard resident. But I'm sure that with your expert help, we'll sail through the Festive Feast course."

"Absolutely! I probably don't have to tell you how excited I am!"

"Well, there's a packed itinerary to get through. Did I mention in my email that a selection of the recipes we'll be demonstrating during the week have been suggested by the residents of Berryford?"

"Really?"

"Every year we hold a fun bake-off competition at the end of November where we ask the villagers to make something that's been handed down from their mothers' or grandmothers' cookery books and the best four recipes are selected to be showcased on that year's Festive Feast cookery course. It's been a great way to involve the whole community in what we're doing here, but it's more than that; it's a way of keeping all the traditional family recipes alive for the next generation – especially the Christmas ones."

Millie's heart gave a nip of surprise when she heard the catch in Claudia's voice and saw a necklace of tears appear along her lower lashes. She hesitated, unsure how to react to the unexpected display of emotion. Although she'd had lots of contact with Claudia since returning from St Lucia, via regular telephone conversations and emails, this was the first time she had met her mentor in the flesh. She didn't want to invade Claudia's privacy, and yet she couldn't ignore her distress.

"Claudia, what's wrong?"

"I'm sorry, Millie. I seem to succumb to tears at the slightest provocation. It's just that the Festive Feast course was the very first one we ran at the cookery school and I think it's the one I will miss the most."

Claudia fished in her sleeve for a tissue to blot away her tears before making a valiant attempt to settle her attractive features into a mask of false bravado.

"So what Tim said is true? This is going to be the last Festive Feast cookery course?"

"Forgive me, Millie. I know you're here to help with the presenting, not to become embroiled in our family politics. I really don't understand why I'm so tearful when I should be seething with anger – although Tim has enough of that for both of us. Why don't you finish your drink and I'll show you to your room, let you get settled in and have an early night. We'll do all our preparations for the course tomorrow, and then there's the tree-lighting ceremony in the village at seven p.m. – yet another tradition that the Berryford residents look forward to each year. If you'd like to come along you'd be very welcome?"

"I'd love to come, Claudia, but... erm, well... this is a little awkward..."

"Oh, don't worry, Zach's invited too! A little Caribbean bird told me about the sparkle of mutual attraction that developed between the two of you whilst you were over in St Lucia!"

Claudia's eyes held Millie's with playful enquiry and her cheeks flooded with heat.

"No, no that's not what I meant! It's just... do you think I could borrow one of your winter coats? In all the rush to get here, I've, well... I've forgotten to pack one."

"Ooops, sorry," laughed Claudia. "No problem. The boot room is through that door over there. We keep a selection of outdoors wear for our cookery school guests to use. Just help yourself to whatever you need. You might also want to avail yourself of a pair of the Wellington boots. I think the forecasters are predicting a fresh deposit of snow tonight. Gosh, I do hope next week's students are able to make it through!"

Claudia led Millie back out to the hallway to collect her suitcase.

"I love this staircase!"

"Oh, I agree! I think it's the best feature of the house. My cousin Dexter and I spent many a happy hour sliding down that bannister when we were younger, much to my grandmother's exasperation. She was right, of course, because sure enough, one Christmas Eve, Dex broke both his wrists after spraying wax polish on his handrail so he could beat me in a race. He's never changed – he still thrives on extreme competition and adrenalin."

Millie noticed Claudia's jaw tighten when she spoke of her cousin, causing her to suspect that her annoyance was related to more than mere childhood antics.

"Here we are. I've given you the Hummingbird Suite. I hope you like it. No prizes for where I got inspiration from," Claudia laughed, striding forward to close the curtains, leaving Millie on the threshold to gaze in wonder at the Caribbean-inspired décor that conjured up such happy memories. "The bathroom is through there. Make yourself at home and I'll see you downstairs at eight a.m. sharp for a quick breakfast before we get stuck in to a full day of culinary fun! Goodnight Millie, and thanks again for coming to our rescue."

"Good night, Claudia."

Millie stood in the middle of the room and performed a three-hundred-and-sixty-degree inspection of the place that would be her home for the next week. The suite was bigger than her whole flat back in London. However, the size had no bearing on her excitement – that was solely down to the fact that there wasn't a splash of magnolia in sight, just a riot of exotic colour and fabric, not to mention her own personal Christmas tree decorated in colourful parrots and baubles in the shape of pineapples and bananas.

Garlands of fuchsia pink, emerald and sky-blue tinsel had been twisted together and draped over the picture frames and there was even a mirrored musical box that played jingle bells when she opened the lid. The headboard, too, had been dressed in brightly coloured bunting and the mantelpiece displayed an impressive collection of painted wooden artefacts from St Lucia, interspersed with a variety of Christmas snow globes. Millie selected a globe containing a miniature replica of the twin Pitons and gave it a vigorous shake, watching with pleasure as the tiny snowflakes descended over their peaks – something that would never happen in real life. The room was her own personal version of paradise and she wondered how Claudia had known what a perfect match it was.

She decided to take a shower to try and wash away the still-lingering odour of dead ferret. The bathroom door was stiff, buckled by the passage of time, and she grinned like a child in a sweet shop when her eyes fell on the black-and-white floor tiles of an oversized chessboard, clearly the Victorian originals. It was a perfect example of a luxury hotel bathroom suite - free-standing roll-top bath, a waterfall shower, even a chaise longue sporting the pyramid of the fluffy white towels guests expected of modern day spas. She almost swooned when she saw the array of bath oils, shampoos and soaps, and stripped off her clothes quickly so she could relish the cascade of hot water on her body.

When she was satisfied that the only fragrance emanating from her skin was that of crushed rose petals, she gave her hair a quick blast with the hairdryer and slipped between the smooth cotton sheets, smiling at the joy of spending the night in a tropical-themed Santa's grotto. Before her thoughts dissolved into dreams, she dawdled briefly on the tasks Claudia had planned for the following morning, but she discovered that what she was most looking forward to was the tree-lighting ceremony and the opportunity to spend more time with Zach.

Chapter Four

The next morning Millie checked the ornate alarm clock on her bedside table and was surprised to see it was only six forty-five. Nevertheless, she was wide awake and craved a fix of caffeine. She threw on a pale blue angora sweater and matching cardigan, collected her beloved scrap box of recipes that went everywhere with her, and galloped down the stairs to the kitchen. She filled the kettle and, while it boiled, took the opportunity of Claudia's absence to scrutinise the culinary amenities more closely.

She slid her palm along the white marble worktops and pristine stainless-steel appliances, before delving into the double-doored refrigerator to discover a true treasure trove of treats which she mentally catalogued for later reference. She loved the central island unit, complete with circular sink and a hi-tech tap which produced instant boiling water at the touch of a button. Resting in the centre was a shiny yellow lever-arch file endorsed with the CC logo containing the laminated recipe cards for each dish to be featured on the Festive Feast course.

Another miniscule Christmas tree loitered in the corner, tastefully bedecked with ornaments in the shape of kitchen utensils; little silver cheese graters, miniature corkscrews, whisks, even a tiny pizza wheel and garlic press. But its quirkily dressed branches, and her bafflement over the mystery of Claudia and Tim's yuletide restraint, paled into insignificant when she saw the view from the window.

Dawn had arrived and with it a brilliant white light highlighting the mounds of snow crowding against the French doors. A languid cascade of snowflakes still tumbled from the flat grey sky and despite being a confirmed sun-worshipper, from her cosy indoor position, Millie was able to recognise the beauty of the winter scenery. Many of the trees circling the house were naked of foliage, their limbs skeletal veins against the pewter-coloured backdrop, yet the greenery of the fir and spruce endured, their brush-like branches topped with a dusting of snow which had fallen from the treetop canopy like powdered sugar. Millie realised the estate must have provided the very trees whose delicious, crushed-pine perfume pervaded the corridors of the house as well as her bedroom.

In the distance, a helix of smoke spun from the chimney of the lodge at the end of the driveway down which she and Zach had travelled the previous afternoon. She knew Zach was an early riser – at least that was something they had in common – although she doubted the reason for his eagerness to greet the day was stubborn insomnia.

Continuing her solo exploration, she cracked open the door at the end of the kitchen and discovered the boot room Claudia had told her about yesterday, home to a medley of Wellington boots, green wax jackets, walking poles and an eclectic assortment of tweed and woolly hats. Millie smiled with relief – clearly former visitors to The Cotswolds Cookery School had also failed to bring their country attire with them.

She fixed herself a cappuccino and grabbed an almond croissant from the enormous walk-in larder. The pastry was buttery and sweet but reminded Millie of her mother and that she would be spending Christmas alone in the south of France. A spasm of guilt invaded her chest. Should she have turned down the chance to co-present the Festive Feast course in favour of a trip to see her family for the holidays?

She shook her head to dispel the sudden onslaught of remorse. When she had told her mother about the switch in arrangements, she had been adamant that Millie should grab the opportunity to spend the week with Claudia and had asked her to email regular photographs and updates with which to wow her Salsa club friends.

Millie drained her coffee in one gulp and placed her empty cup into the sink. She brushed the scattered flakes of pastry from the counter top and trotted out to the hallway to explore further. She had only taken a couple of steps when her toe connected with a loose wire and she fell headlong onto the polished parquet flooring, skidding along on her stomach to the bottom of the stairs like an Olympic skeleton racer. She sat up and rubbed her knee and elbow to disperse the pain, squinting into the gloom to see what had breached her path. Snaking along the floor was a coil of cable from the Christmas tree lights. Her lips cracked into a rueful expression until she saw Claudia rushing down the stairs to help her up.

"Millie, what happened? Are you okay?"

"I'm fine. It's totally my fault. I wasn't looking where I was going – something I have a habit of doing, I'm afraid."

"Thank goodness. Come on, let's get you a coffee. Did you sleep well?"

"Like a yuletide log!" laughed Millie, as Claudia linked her arm and guided her back into the kitchen where she fixed them a cafetière and slotted the arch-lever file of recipes under her arm.

"Why don't we take our coffees into the library? Tim got a fabulous fire going before he retreated to his workshop muttering something about working on a remote-control switch for the tree-lighting ceremony tonight."

"Oh, yes, please," smiled Millie, anxious to take a peek at her host's sanctuary.

She followed Claudia across the hallway towards the library, this time taking care not to trip. An aroma of furniture polish, stale cigar smoke and nostalgia assaulted Millie's senses as soon as she entered the room – a veritable cathedral of culinary literature and the place where Claudia had written all her cookery books. She chose a seat on the wrinkled Chesterfield sofa and Claudia perched on the edge of the wing-backed chair next to her.

"So, the way I've designed the Festive Feast itinerary is that on Monday we'll make an early start and showcase a sumptuous Christmas breakfast which we can enjoy together afterwards. On Tuesday we'll be preparing a mid-morning brunch, Wednesday it's the star attraction of Christmas lunch, then Thursday it's a festive version of Afternoon Tea, and finally, on Friday, we'll be creating the canapés for the farewell drinks party."

Claudia opened the file and handed Millie a recipe for chickpea and cumin croquettes with a glossy photograph attached. She could almost smell the Indian spices and garlic waft through the air and her mouth watered in anticipation.

"Everything on the menu has been triple-tested apart from the four winning recipes from the villagers' competition which is what we'll be doing today. We have mini orange-marmalade roulades with dark chocolate ganache from Mrs Dartington who runs the village post office, and cranberry-and-white chocolate muffins baked in tiny terracotta pots with chocolate antlers stuck into the brandy buttercream topping, both of which we'll be including in the High Tea tutorial on Thursday. Then there's the egg and smoked salmon savoury cupcakes served in extra-large egg cups created by Old Mrs Greenwood, and the fourth and final recipe is a fabulous selection of sweet mince samosas designed by Mrs Singh who's the secretary of the local WI. I thought we could also make a few batches of my grandmother's special-recipe gingerbread and then we can take everything down to the village hall for the party after the tree-lighting ceremony."

"Sounds like my idea of a perfect day," sighed Millie. "How many enthusiastic foodies are you expecting for the Festive Feast course?"

"Eight. Two men and two women from the same law firm in London and their respective spouses. Leo Groves, the senior partner, and his wife Gina, have rented a cottage in St Ives for Christmas and they want to surprise their family with a gastronomic banquet made by their own fair hands on Christmas day. The others just want to brush up on their skills and have some fun away from the daily grind to six o'clock."

"What time are they arriving?"

"Around five this afternoon. Gina said they were all delighted to accept our invitation to take part in the tree-lighting ceremony so that should give them enough time to settle into their suites and wrap up warm before we make our way down to the village green."

Claudia paused to flick her hair behind her ears, revealing a pair of chunky red earrings in the shape of poinsettia leaves that complimented her cream-and-scarlet silk scarf that she'd tied in a complicated knot at her neck. Millie glanced down at her own attire and cringed when a voice - very much like Zach's - commented on her lack of appreciation for the season. She really must ask Tim if she could borrow a couple of his jazzy golf jumpers if she was planning on leaving the house at all during the next week.

"Oh, who's that ringing? It's barely eight a.m.! Back in a minute. Why don't you check through Mrs Greenwood's recipe for the savoury cupcakes and see what you think?"

"Sure."

Millie ran her eyes down the hand-written recipe and smiled when she saw it was in pounds and ounces. Nevertheless, if the end result was as delicious as the instructions sounded, they would be onto to a winner. She replaced the precious scrap of paper in the plastic folder and decided to explore the bibliographic paradise whilst she waited for Claudia to finish her phone call.

She padded across the colourful Persian rug to the bookshelf next to the fireplace, her heart pounding in anticipation of what she was about to discover. Books of all shapes and sizes had been crammed onto shelves lining three sides of the room. The fourth was made up of a pair of floor-to-ceiling windows overlooking the vast expanse of lawn at the front of the property, complete with upholstered seats where any ardent bookworm could while away the hours with their chosen literary indulgence.

She ran her fingertips across the protruding spines like the keys on a piano and smiled. To Millie, all books provided a portal into another world: but only cookery books could guide the reader in the art of moulding seemingly disparate ingredients into taste-bud-zinging perfection.

The library at Stonelea Manor was no ordinary library, more a cornucopia of brightly-coloured gems waiting to be explored, to be freed from the prison of the shelf and their contents brought to life in the kitchen. There were cookery books Millie had not known existed; more a narrative comment on society at the time of writing than instruction on food preparation. Some were well-thumbed, the best friends of the busy professional cook, others pristine. Some were a single copy, while others were represented in multiple editions, updated over the years. The diversity of the published subject matter amazed her. There were books in many different languages, some with glossy photographs, some without. Each book contained a nugget of hidden treasure, promising an insight into what keeps body and soul together in their corner of the world.

She selected a book at random – *for how could she possibly be expected to choose?* – and was just about to turn the page when she heard the door creak open. She looked up to see Claudia, her apricot lips pursed, and her forehead creased with anxiety. Two spots of colour highlighted her cheeks and her hand trembled as she fingered one of her earrings.

"Claudia? What's wrong?"

To Millie's surprise, Claudia burst into tears and she rushed across the room to her side.

"I really don't know why I'm crying. It's not as though this hasn't happened before!"

"What's happened before?"

"That was Leo Groves on the phone. One of the women in his party is six months pregnant and her husband doesn't want to risk driving from Kent to the Cotswolds in this weather. Their friends have decided to stay in Kent with them, so that means only Leo and Gina, and Mike and Marianne will be joining us this afternoon. I know I should have taken Tim's advice and cancelled the course before we accepted any bookings, but as it was going to be the last one, I really wanted to make it the most fabulous one ever." Claudia's tears returned and this time she let them flow unabated, heaving in lungfuls of air as she allowed her emotions to run free.

Millie squeezed Claudia's hands and gave her the space to recover her composure in her own time. Concern whipped through her brain, and again a myriad of questions about what was going on with the cookery school's future nibbled at her curiosity. But they could wait. What Claudia needed was something to divert her attention and Millie had the perfect solution. It was what she always did when life tossed a random grenade in her path.

"Come on, I think a session of extreme baking is what we need."

Claudia smiled, her strikingly green eyes lighting up immediately. "Agreed!"

Millie grabbed the file of recipes and followed Claudia back to the kitchen. She unfolded one of the cookery school's logoed aprons and tied the strings securely around her waist.

"Right. What shall we bake first?"

"I think it has to be my grandmother's gingerbread recipe smothered in lots of lemon icing. After all, that's what started everything off at the Claudia Croft Cotswold Cookery School, and the Berryford tree lighting ceremony wouldn't be the same without it – paired with a mug of hot chocolate laced with brandy."

Claudia placed a huge silver soup pan on the hob and got busy adding catering-sized tins of golden syrup and treacle to the melting butter and sugar, stirring the contents with a wooden spoon. "Look, there's the original recipe for the gingerbread."

Instead of handing her a sheet of paper containing hand-written instructions, Claudia pointed to a framed picture on the wall that Millie hadn't noticed before. She strode over to take a closer look.

"Gran wrote it on the back of a Christmas card that my Grandfather gave her when they were courting in the nineteen forties," explained Claudia, her eyes sparkling under the glare of the overhead lights. "The party in the village hall after the tree-lighting ceremony has become a sort of village tradition, where everyone contributes something from their own family's recipe book, or they make the decorations or the spiced punch, or help with the music, or give people taxi rides home afterwards. It's become a real community thing – this year the children from the local primary school are coming to sing a few carols. It was after one of these nights, ten years ago, that Tim had the idea of opening a cookery school at the manor, and the rest, as they say, is history."

When the gingerbread was safely in the oven and producing intoxicating aromas of spicy ginger and warm sticky treacle, Claudia and Millie set to work preparing the orange marmalade for the roulades and the brandy-flavoured buttercream for the muffins. They took a short break for lunch before resuming with the sweet mince samosas, which Millie's loved, and the savoury cupcakes.

"Wow, these eggs are really fresh! Look at the colour of the yolks!"

"I get them from Jim Garitty's farm. I try to source local produce for all the cookery school's menus as much as possible, as well as using the local services. That's why we run the annual competition to find four family recipes to feature on each one of the courses on the Festive Feasts itinerary, with Gran's gingerbread taking the fifth spot as one of the sweet canapes. It's the perfect way to keep the old recipes alive. In the new year, Tim and I collate them into a booklet to sell for charity. We now have forty recipes and I was hoping to pull in a few favours at my publishers and have a book published, but I'm not sure that's going to happen now."

"Claudia, why…

Claudia had just slid the last tray of the egg and smoked salmon savouries into the oven when there was tinkle on the doorbell.

"Ah, that'll be Leo and Gina, and their friends Mike and Marianne. Would you mind decorating the gingerbread slices with those edible holly leaves whilst I show them up to their rooms?"

"No problem," smiled Millie, resigned to the fact that the mystery of the school's impending closure would continue for a while longer. Maybe she could corner Tim and ask him about it.

Claudia reached over to give Millie's forearm a quick squeeze. "Thank you, Millie… for everything." And then she dashed from the kitchen to greet her guests.

Millie took a moment to survey the kitchen for the first time that day and what she saw didn't surprise her in the least. The area that Claudia had been working in was as pristine as when they had started; tidy work-tops, utensils washed, dried, and returned to their respective homes, the ingredients they had finished with returned to their respective shelves in the larder. Whereas, despite her strenuous efforts to corral her clutter demons, Millie's side of the kitchen looked like a scene from the Cotswolds Culinary Catastrophe. Although, in order not to douse herself in too much despondency, she had to admit that she had seen far worse and she resolved to thank Poppy for her contri-bution to her progress as it was obviously producing results – albeit with a long, long way to go.

She gathered everything together, loaded the industrial-sized dishwasher and slammed the door shut. She inhaled the enticing aroma of cooling gingerbread and set about decorating the squares with tiny sugar paste holly leaves and red berries and arranging everything on huge silver platters to transport to the village hall in good time for the switching-on of the lights.

The old Millie would have left the remaining crockery and cutlery in the sink, but the new improved Millie located a pair of Marigolds, filled a bowl with soapy water, and set to washing down the benches and buffing up the silver coffee machine that had been splashed with brandy buttercream and a splodge of something green and gooey she didn't recognise. She didn't pause until every last spatula was resting contentedly in its allocated spot.

An image of a suitably-impressed Zach floated across her mind, with Millie centre-stage as she presented the kitchen to him like a showroom sales assistant keen to earn that month's bonus. A spasm of electricity shot through her chest and headed southwards when she remembered that she would be seeing him in a couple of hours in Berryford.

Chapter Five

"Tim, if we don't leave now we'll miss the show!" sighed Claudia as she watched her husband slot yet another screwdriver into the already jam-packed rucksack he had insisted on bringing with him to the tree-lighting ceremony '*just in case*'.

"It always pays to be prepared, darling," replied Tim, his forehead creased in thought. "Remember last year when George Stanton blew up the kettle and everyone was forced to drink mulled wine and Christmas punch instead of tea and coffee? The whole evening descended into an absolutely riot!"

"And it was the best Christmas party the village has ever had!" laughed Claudia, leaning forward to deposit a kiss on Tim's cheek before linking his arm and steering him towards the front door. "Come on."

"Do you think I should take a spare roll of gaffer tape?"

"No!"

"What do you think, Millie? Isn't it better to be over-prepared than risk the regret of a forgotten gadget?"

"Erm, I'm not sure," she hedged, uncertain how to answer such a loaded question. It was the first time she'd met Tim and she liked him on the spot, her heart flooding with empathy for her fellow clutter-collector, especially when she saw the pleading expression scrawled across his handsome face. "Maybe."

"I'll take that as a yes then!"

And before anyone could stop him, he'd cantered off back to his workshop to collect even more essential tools, leaving the two women rolling their eyes and giggling on the doorstep until he reappeared, stooped under the weight of his over-laden rucksack like a DIY-obsessed Father Christmas.

It was clear to Millie that Tim belonged to the eccentric part of the people spectrum. Dressed in a hand-knitted sweater, incongruously depicting only the rear end of a reindeer, he was as far from Millie's image of a high-flying City architect as it was possible to get. However, his silver eyes held a sharp intelligence that reflected an avid interest in everything around him and he exuded energy, almost as if he was getting ready to embark on a sprint. His hair, more salt than pepper, was thick and luxuriant and cut into a trendy style by the local French hairdresser, and the fine lines around his mouth spoke of regular laughter. Time spent with Tim Croft would be the highlight of anyone's day.

He insisted on driving them to Berryford in his Range Rover which made short work of the snow-covered roads. Thankfully, the temperature had climbed during the day to hover just above freezing. The covering of snow remained, but rivulets of water were trickling in the gutters and the absence of a breeze made the night air much more appealing.

As soon as Claudia emerged from the passenger seat, she was mobbed by friends and neighbours and dragged off to inspect the Christmas tree and pronounce her delight at the villagers' foodie offerings. Tim shrugged his shoulders in familiar resignation, relieved her of her platters of gingerbread and accompanied Millie into the village hall where he too was summonsed for his opinion on the generator that was being used to power the lights.

Left alone, Millie experienced a spasm of awkwardness, but it didn't last long. No one was allowed to feel like an outsider in Berryford, especially during the festivities. She set down the platter of dark chocolate roulades on an old wallpaper table alongside the most elegantly dressed Christmas cake she had ever seen. A Calypso-style version of *Jingle*

Bells blared out from a pair of huge loudspeakers on the stage at the far end of the room next to an eclectically decorated silver tinsel tree. The whole room smelled of cloves, cinnamon and happy times, with just the faintest hint of bleach, and was clearly a beacon of light in the heart of the village.

"Hi, Millie. Looks like you and Claudia have been busy today. There's enough food here to feed a whole battalion of Christmas elves!" declared Zach as he carefully lowered a keg of beer from his shoulder on to the makeshift bar that was crammed with a kaleidoscope of spirits ranging from the standard whisky and gin to the more exotic like the thick green liquor that Millie thought must be Crème de Menthe – something she had last seen in her French grandmother's drinks cabinet when she was a child!

"We have! And you're right – there's a mountain of goodies on offer, but we had to use up so many ingredients in the larder because four of the Festive Feast guests have had to cancel at the last minute. Only two couples are enrolled on the Christmas cookery course this time. Look, over there next to the piano; that's Leo Groves and his wife, Gina, and his business partner, Mike Sanderson and his wife, Marianne."

Zach followed the direction of Millie's eyes to where Gina and Marianne were sampling the mulled wine, their mouths stretching into a grimace when the high alcohol content hit the back of their throats. Mike rolled his eyes at his friends and took a sip too, then promptly descended into a coughing fit, his tortoise-shell glasses slipping from his face and blonde quiff quivering in the onslaught as Marianne gamely patted his back whilst trying to hold back a bout of giggles.

Leo, clearly the more sensible of the group, shook his head when Gina offered him her glass and instead selected a bottle of beer which he clutched to his chest as if his life depended on it. He certainly fit his name perfectly, thought Millie, as she took in his broad, rugby-honed shoulders, the tight auburn curls and the bump on the bridge of his nose to indicate he had been in the wars – albeit on a sports pitch. He radiated self-assurance and Millie knew she would have no qualms choosing Leo Groves to act on her behalf should she ever find herself in the unfortunate position of having to instruct a solicitor.

"Hey, you two! What are you doing loitering in here?" called Tim through the doorway. "The ceremony is about to start!

"Come on."

Zach guided Millie to the village green where everyone and their dog had congregated, bundled into thick layers and the most diverse collection of woolly hats she had ever seen. Some sported the expected pom-poms, others a variety of animal ears with one elderly lady modelling a tall, pointed, multi-coloured unicorn horn that was the envy of several little girls who were staring up at the headgear in wide-eyed fascination.

The village brass band finished their somewhat off-key version of *Deck the Halls* to a smattering of appreciative applause, then struck up the first bars of *O Christmas Tree* and a choir of schoolchildren began their well-rehearsed rendition of the traditional overture to the tree-lighting ceremony. Their young voices, so innocent, clear and full of hope and excitement for the approaching visit of Santa Claus, caused a lump to form in Millie's throat.

Dragging her emotions back into their box, she continued her sweep of the gathering surrounding the mammoth tree and couldn't help but smile. Enclosed by a white picket fence, the tree was magnificent, draped in strings of fairy lights awaiting the spark of life, and a necklace of tinsel with a gold star adorning its crown. However, Millie noticed that its branches were strangely devoid of decorations. A family of flashing reindeers provided the only source of light, apart from the lanterns the well-organised had brought with them and the tiny lights pinned to the top of the musician's stands.

As the final bars of the carol melted into the night, Tim and Claudia stepped from the shadows and climbed onto a small makeshift platform to a raucous welcome of whoops and whistles. Millie laughed as the image on Tim's Christmas sweater suddenly made complete sense. Claudia had removed her padded jacket to reveal the other half of the reindeer knitted onto the front of her own jumper - the head, the antlers and the huge red pom-pom nose of Rudolph - which completed the animal when she stood next to her husband causing a trickle of laughter from the crowd.

"Claudia and I would like to welcome everyone to the thirty-third Berryford tree-lighting ceremony. You will have noticed that this year's tree is much larger than our previous trees. For obvious reasons, we wanted this night to be the best ever. Before I ask the winner of the school raffle to step up and turn on the lights, I just wanted to take this opportunity to say a few thank yous."

Tim paused, his Adam's apple working overtime, and Millie was surprised to hear a wobble in his voice. He had removed his hat and his hair stuck out in random tufts, made worse by his constant habit of running his fingers from root to tip.

"First, my thanks to Martha Jones for her superb organisational skills. Once again, she has ensured that everything has gone according to plan for our annual celebration of Christmas cheer, even to the extent of ordering the weather gods to press the pause button on the snow we've been experiencing these last couple of days. Secondly, I want to thank everyone who has contributed to the wonderful spread waiting for us in the village hall, and the fabulous Berryford Band and the primary school choir for entertaining us with their amazing voices."

There followed a crescendo of applause and stamping of feet in agreement.

"Finally, Claudia and I just want to say a huge heartfelt thank you for all the support you have shown us both over the years – we couldn't have done any of it without your help, your encouragement and your fabulous produce. It means everything to us."

Millie watched as Claudia moved over to take Tim's hand and flick a tear from the side of her cheek. She was desperate to unravel the mystery of what was going on with Stonelea Manor because if this was Tim's annual Christmas speech, it was more akin to a goodbye eulogy. She glanced up at Zach, and saw that his eyes were fixed on Tim, his jaw set, his expression serious. What was going on?

"So, Happy Christmas everyone… and it gives me great pleasure to invite Sasha Dennison to help

Claudia and I to switch on this year's Christmas tree lights."

Sasha's grandparents led the beaming five-year-old onto the stage where she was endowed with a badge the size of a saucer depicting a snowman wearing a Santa hat. Tim stooped down to collect a weird looking contraption sporting a large round red button – clearly one of his inventions – and held it towards Sasha whose eyes were dancing with excitement at being selected to do the honours. She lowered her mittened hand with great glee and the tree's lights sprang into life to a rumble of oohs and aahs.

The choir burst into song once more, their voices lifting into the air as they reached the high notes of *We Wish You A Merry Christmas*, whilst the crowd moved en masse to form an orderly queue around the perimeter of the picket fence.

"What's happening?" asked Millie, clapping her hands to get some feeling into her fingers.

"Well, I'm not sure whether you noticed, but the tree is naked!" laughed Zach, his eyes crinkling attractively at the corners as he looked down at her, sending a pleasant zip of electricity through her veins.

"Yes, I did think that was a bit strange."

"Well, that's because as part of this weekend's festivities, everyone either makes their own decoration, or choses one from their family's collection that means something special to them, and hangs it on the tree as a dedication to someone they've lost this year and want to include in the celebration. Here, I thought you might like this."

Zach reached into the pocket of his jacket, pulled out a bundle of gold-flecked tissue paper, and handed it over to Millie, an unfathomable expression in his eyes.

"What is it?"

"Open it and see."

She stared at him for a few seconds, her heart sending signals of anticipation cavorting around her chest as she wondered what the parcel contained. When they were in St Lucia, she had confided in Zach about the loss of her father when she was a teenager, and he obviously hadn't forgotten – had even thought to supply her with a token of remembrance to hang on the village tree.

She swallowed down on her emotions as they peeked over the rim of their carefully crafted confinement, and gently peeled back the paper to reveal an intricately carved wooden star painted in silver and threaded with a bright red ribbon. A whoosh of gratitude rushed through her veins as an image of her father, laughing at one of Monique's more outrageous Salsa costumes, floated across her mind's eye and tears sparkled at her lower lashes.

"Did you... did you make this yourself?"

"I did."

"It's beautiful," she managed to whisper. "Thank you, Zach."

Zach produced a gel pen and held it out. "I thought you could write your dad's name on the ribbon," he added, gently.

"Yes. Yes, I think I will."

Millie took the pen and in her best hand-writing she wrote *Always in my thoughts, Forever in my heart* before taking her place in the queue to hang the ornament on the most luxuriant branch she could find. A wave of sorrow surged through her body and she took a few minutes to grapple with her memories by inspecting some of the other Christmas tree decorations, to read the names of those past residents of Berryford who had been loved and were missing from that night's celebrations but whose spirits were still alive amongst them.

What a fabulous tradition, she thought, sending up a missive of affection to her father who, as a lover of any excuse for a party, she knew would be looking down on them that evening. She resolved to ask Claudia if she would reclaim the gift when the tree was dismantled in the new year and send it on to her in London.

She was about to tell Zach how apt his present was – her father had been an avid astronomer and the Chair of the local astronomical society before he died – when they were interrupted by a shout from a tall, slender guy who had eschewed the tradition of Christmas-themed attire in favour of figure-hugging designer jeans and what was clearly a very expensive ivory cashmere sweater.

"Hey, Zach, if you don't get inside sharpish, all the delicious goodies will have been hoovered up by the ravenous revellers!"

With neatly gelled ebony hair, the newcomer looked like he had just stepped off the front page of GQ magazine, and his arrival at their sides was accompanied by a swirl of fragrance that hung in the air like a nuclear fallout cloud. In fact, his cologne was so strong that Millie had to conceal a cough under the guise of a robust throat-clearing session. Zach bent down to whisper in Millie's ear, his action so intimate that the warmth of his breath on her cheek sent shivers of delight through her body.

"Blake does tend to go a bit overboard with the aftershave, always has."

"A bit!" she giggled.

"Any news, Zach?"

To her surprise, Millie felt Zach's whole body stiffen as he considered his reply to Blake's question and she scrutinised his face for an indication as to the reason for it. Not another secret, she sighed to herself.

"Nothing yet. Blake, can I introduce you to Amelia Harper? She's co-presenting the Festive Feast course at Stonelea Manor with Claudia this year."

"Delighted!" beamed Blake, his smooth, tanned features morphing into a smile.

"Hi, Blake. It's great to meet you. Please, call me Millie."

Before she knew what was happening, Millie was engulfed in a hearty bear hug of a welcome and received a fresh blast of cologne for her trouble. When she was released she saw the glint of mischief dancing in Blake's chocolate-brown eyes as he flicked a quick glance at Zach before giving her a very obvious once-over. A chuckle rumbled at the back of her throat, but she managed to hold on.

"Darling, it's just so good to finally be able to put a face to the name. Zach talks about you *all the time* and now I understand why. She's gorgeous, Zach. I totally get why you've been keeping her to yourself!"

Zach rolled his eyes, but the tenseness of his earlier demeanour softened to accept the jovial ribbing.

"Blake, Millie is…"

"Well, I'll leave you two lovebirds to cuddle up under the mistletoe. There's a Pina Colada shouting my name at the bar. Don't you just adore those little parrot cocktail sticks Claudia brought back from St Lucia? Oh, and don't forget to introduce Millie to one of Kate's famous mince pies before they all disappear. Of course, I shan't be indulging myself." Blake patted his washboard flat stomach. "Got a slinky little number for the New Year's Ball that I want to dazzle everyone with and it most certainly won't look at its best with unsightly bulges! Perhaps I'll see you in the café, Millie, before you scoot off back to that crazy metropolis that is our capital city."

"Yes, I hope so." Millie grinned, already feeling a Blake-sized friendship bubble ballooning in her chest.

"I like this one, Zach. Play your cards right and maybe this year won't be all bad news!"

Blake winked lasciviously at Zach, anointed Millie with another wide, neon-bright smile, and trotted off towards the village hall leaving a fresh burst of Chanel Monsieur in his wake.

"Come on. I could do with something to warm me up."

The village hall buzzed with activity accompanied by a cacophony of animated conversation interspersed with laughter and the occasional burst of song. Millie accepted a glass of warm, spice-infused punch, slotting her fingers through the handle of the glass mug and inhaling the delicious aroma of all-things Christmassy. She performed a swift stocktake of the room and picked out Claudia and Tim standing next to the stage, being treated like guests of honour, and noticed that for the first time since she had arrived in Berryford, the furrows on Claudia's forehead had melted away and she looked happy and relaxed.

Gina, Mike and Marianne had sensibly swapped the punch for beer and were busy devouring the chocolate roulades as though they were worried that their stay at Stonelea Manor involved a restrictive health spa regime instead of a sumptuous culinary feast! Gina and Marianne's heads were thrown back in laughter at something Leo was saying and Millie suspected that the switch to beer may have come a little too late.

Both women presented a sleek, elegant and polished image, their hair freshly coiffed by their favourite Kensington hairdresser especially for their week's stay in rural Gloucestershire; Gina's a short, cropped bob the colour of sunshine that emphasised her strong cheekbones, Marianne's a long mane of curls that wouldn't have looked out of place in a Titian painting. Their cheeks were rosy from the heat of the room after the icy breeze at the tree lighting ceremony, but they looked like they had slotted into village life perfectly.

"Excuse me for a minute." Zach squeezed her arm and made his way across the room to help a ginger-haired teenager change the huge beer barrel that had started to spill its precious contents on the floor.

"Gorgeous, isn't he?" murmured Blake, nudging her in the ribs as he sipped from the rim of his Pina Colada, his eyes fixed firmly on Zach's taut buttocks currently raised high in the air as he struggled to attach the nozzle. "I think I'll miss him the most, you know."

"What do you mean?" Millie shot a look at Blake, hopeful that at last she was about to be informed about what was going on.

"Well, I don't think vacancies for estate managers are two-a-penny around here, do you? When I saw Zach's mother at the café yesterday she mentioned something about him relocating permanently to the Caribbean. I suppose it's better than the heather-strewn glens of Scotland! Who in their right mind would want to live there?" grimaced Blake, his cute ski-slope nose wrinkling as if Scotland was in Outer Space. "I mean, do they even have Waitrose? And don't even get me started on the quality of the wifi!"

Blake performed a theatrical shiver that caused Millie to giggle despite the cauldron of emotions his disclosures had whipped up inside her. Zach was moving back to St Lucia? Why hadn't he told her?

"I'm sure Scotland has entered the twenty-first century with the rest of us."

"Maybe, darling, but you can count me out for regular weekend visits – although it might be worth a jaunt just to check out those fabulous kilts the men insist on wearing. And whilst a trip to the Caribbean would be a totally different scenario – I have absolutely no problem with a splash of Rum and Relaxation – the airfare is sadly beyond my meagre means."

Blake wandered off to replenish his drink with a generous dose of neat Bacardi, leaving Millie to absorb what his revelations about Zach's future meant. Like Blake, there was no way she could afford a flight to St Lucia unless Claudia booked her services to present another one of the Paradise Cookery School courses – which in effect meant that once he'd left she would probably never see Zach again.

The thought caused a burst of panic to explode in her chest, followed swiftly by an intense desire to seek him out and demand that he explain what was going on. Why hadn't he said anything to her? Was this the reason for the change in the tone of his texts before she left London and why he'd said they had 'a lot to talk about'? Obviously, he was going to tell her that there could be no future for them if they lived in different countries, and her reaction to this made her realise that her feelings for Zach had morphed beyond friendship into something entirely different and much more worrying. After what had happened with Luke, she had no desire to revisit the heartache that losing someone close caused, and the only way to do that was to surround herself with a sturdy armour of detachment.

But could she do that? She wasn't sure she was capable of controlling the way she felt when Zach was at her side. Why did her relationships always have to be so complicated?

Millie drained her glass, running her tongue around her lips to collect the last taste of cinnamon, and she suddenly realised that the village hall had almost emptied. As it was a school day the next morning, everyone with children had ushered them from the party with promises of hot chocolate and marshmallows when they got home, and Tim and Claudia were waved off like newlyweds to a fanfare of thanks and farewells and with numerous beautifully wrapped gifts under their arms.

She sighed and made her way to the kitchen, having agreed to stay behind to help with the tidying up, but her offer hadn't been entirely altruistic – whatever was going on at Stonelea Manor, she wanted to get to the bottom of it. Yes, Tim had told her that this year's Festive Feast course would be the last one, but why did the scaling back, or even the closure, of the cookery school business affect Zach's position as the estate manager?

The only way to find out was to ask him directly and brace herself for the answer she didn't want him to give – that Blake had spoken the truth. Zach was leaving the UK for a new life in St Lucia and she was devastated.

Chapter Six

Zach drove his car through the stone pillars and onto the driveway that led to Stonelea Manor. A whoosh of relief flashed through Millie's body when she saw that the tarmac was clear. Although it was still cold, it was the middle of December after all, the temperature had lifted and the only snow that remained was the undisturbed blanket of white spread across the front lawns.

When they arrived in the gravelled car park at the back of the house, Zach cut the engine and twisted round to face her. It was eleven thirty and she was bone-tired from a hectic day she had spent baking up a storm with Claudia, then scrubbing the kitchen in the village hall, not to mention the soporific effect of the three glasses of punch she had devoured, each successive glass tasting better than the last for some reason. Her head felt heavy and all she really wanted to do was dash into the boot room, peel off the padded green jacket she had borrowed and shoot up those magnificent stairs to bed because she had an early start the next morning and she needed to feel fresh and raring to go for the first day of the course.

However, she had resolved to find out what was going on. She didn't feel she could ask Claudia who'd had ample opportunity to share her problems with Millie, and had chosen not to, and anyway, she doubted there would be a single moment of privacy to discuss such delicate matters, even if their numbers *were* depleted. She had no idea when she would be seeing Zach next and she could see that the kitchen was suffused in darkness which meant Claudia and Tim and their guests had retired for the night and they would have the place to themselves.

"Come and have a night cap. There's Blue Mountain coffee, or we could indulge in a tot of Tim's single malt, if you prefer?"

"Millie, I…"

"Please Zach."

Before she was waylaid by arguments to the contrary, she shot from the car and into the house. She could envisage Zach's reaction to a tee – the eye roll, the sigh, the twist of his lips into a resigned smirk, but he followed her into the kitchen nonetheless.

Millie set the kettle to boil and lit a couple of cathedral candles, only subsequently realising that Zach might have thought she had more romantic intentions in mind. The kitchen filled with flickering golden light and once again Millie was surprised at the lack of Christmas decorations in the room where it was intended that their guests would spend the majority of their time. It was another mystery she would just have to add to the lengthening list because her brain felt like it had been stuffed with cotton wool.

She carried the coffee mugs, and a plate of home-made mince pies, to the table next to the French doors and sat down facing Zach, determined to excavate the details as to the cause of Claudia's distress, Tim's anger, and Blake's despondency at Zach's imminent flight.

"Okay, what's going on with the cookery school?"

"I don't know what..."

"Don't fob me off. I know it's none of my business, but I care about Claudia. I know how much she loves the cookery school and I can see how upset she is that this year's Christmas tutorials are going to be the last. She's trying to hide it, but it's not working, and Tim spends all his time hiding out in his workshop, bashing away his resentment on those inventions of his. Whatever it is, it's more than just the Festive Feast course, though, because even Blake is miserable and that isn't a character trait I would associate with him. Please, Zach, tell me what's going on."

Zach sighed, a muscle in his jaw working overtime as he took a couple of beats to master his emotions. He swallowed a long draught of his black coffee to inject a little courage into his veins, inhaled a deep breath, and met Millie's eyes.

"It's true. The Claudia Croft Cookery School is closing its doors at the end of the week."

"But why? Every course is sold out as soon as it goes online."

"It's amazingly successful! That's why Claudia and Tim decided to set up The Paradise Cookery School at their villa in St Lucia."

"Then I don't understand. Is Claudia closing that too?"

Millie's heart pounded out a symphony of sadness as she contemplated all the hard work she and Ella had put into finalising the school. Claudia had confided in her that it was a long-held dream to upgrade the plantation house into a luxury boutique hotel so that their guests could stay on site whilst learning the secrets of gastronomic excellence Caribbean-style.

"No. The Paradise Cookery School is safe. Claudia and Tim will probably relocate there."

"So, what will happen to Stonelea Manor?"

Ah, there it was, thought Millie, she had hit the jackpot with that question.

"It'll probably be sold."

"Sold! Are you serious? The estate has been in Claudia's family for three generations."

"True."

Zach took another sip of his coffee, then ran his fingers through his hair causing it stand up in those attractive tufts Millic thought were so cute. However, the serious expression on his face upset her tremendously as she put two-and-two together after her conversation with Blake and realised what the sale of the manor to a new owner would mean for Zach's future livelihood.

"I can't believe Claudia and Tim want to sell."

"They don't."

"Then why?"

"It's complicated."

"I'm listening."

Now that she had Zach sitting in front of her, she wasn't going to be fobbed off until she had heard the full story, no matter how long it took or how hard her exhaustion pulled at her bones. She comforted herself with the contention that it wasn't as though she was sticking her nose into Claudia and Tim's private business because Blake knew what was going on, and so it seemed did most of the residents of Berryford after the way they had made such a fuss over them that evening – they were leaving the village!

She could feel the pessimistic vibes emanating from Zach which shocked her to the core. He had never been anything other than upbeat and positive, continually cheering her on from the side-lines as she emerged from her self-imposed sojourn of gloom after the debacle with Luke. Now the tables had been turned and it was her turn to come to *his* rescue, but she had no idea how – she didn't own a country estate that required his unique services. However, she was beginning to understand why the last text message she'd received in London had changed tone.

"Zach?" she pressed.

"Okay, okay. I think Claudia has already told you that Stonelea Manor was purchased by her grandfather who preferred to live the life of a country gentleman rather than a City wheeler-and-dealer on the stock market where he made his money. When he died, he left the house to his two sons, Claudia's father, Charles, and her uncle, David. David wasn't interested in the estate and when his son Dexter was twelve, they emigrated to Australia.

"When Charles passed away, Claudia inherited his half share of the Stonelea estate, and similarly when her uncle David died, his share passed to Dexter so they ended up owning the Manor equally. Like his father, Dexter had no interest in a crumbling old building on the other side of the world, so when Claudia decided to set up her cookery school ten years ago, he raised no objections, and was content to be a silent partner in return for a proportion of the profits as rent."

Millie remembered Claudia talking about her cousin, reminiscing about their escapades in the grounds and the incident when he had carelessly raced down the banister and broken his wrists. She suspected there was more than just bones that Dexter had broken recently.

"In July, Dexter contacted Claudia and Tim to ask if they would buy his share of the house. Tim told me that Dexter has always been a bit cavalier when it came to investing his father's money and this time he'd chosen a start-up mining company that promised fabulous returns but, of course, didn't deliver. Anyway, his creditors are screaming for their cash and the only asset he has left to sell is his half share of Stonelea Manor."

Zach replaced his coffee mug on the silver tray and arranged the teaspoons into neat lines. Millie said nothing, not wanting to interrupt his monologue.

"Of course, Claudia and Tim had bought the villa in St Lucia and all their cash was tied up in the renovations which didn't come cheap. They tried to raise funds using the manor as security, but another blow fell when the bank's surveyor advised them that they would probably need to replace the roof in the next two years – so no chance of a mortgage and the only option left is to sell. Claudia's devastated, of course, but has tried to look at the situation from Dexter's point of view, insisting he has every right to liquidate his share. I know it's not my place to say this, but I think all this worry is the cause of her recent tiredness."

"What does Tim think of Dexter's ultimatum?"

"Tim is livid with Dexter for springing this on them, but he's the most sensible, pragmatic guy I know. He's managed to spin the whole nightmare into a positive and has almost persuaded Claudia that they will be much happier living in St Lucia where she'll be able to concentrate on building up the Paradise Cookery School, put the finishing touches to the hotel, and producing the high-grade cocoa from the trees she's been cultivating. What's really upsetting Claudia is how the sale will affect the wider community. Stonelea Manor has been at the centre of many of the villagers' lives for decades, and she treats everyone as part of the family – and you've seen tonight how her friendship is reciprocated."

Millie's heart squeezed painfully when she saw the ragged despair on Zach's face. Claudia and Tim already had an estate manager in St Lucia, would they really need two? But there was something else lingering in Zach's eyes and she knew he hadn't yet finished his explanation.

"And?"

Zach met her eyes and Millie held her breath as he prepared to divulge the sting in the story's tail.

"Last week, Dexter informed Tim that he's bringing a potential purchaser to have a look round the estate on Thursday and suddenly it all seems much more urgent and real."

Millie allowed this last nugget of information to sink into her brain, joining up the dots until she understood what Blake had meant when he had asked Zach if he had any news. If the buyer was interested, Zach was going to be out of a job sooner rather than later. But surely the new owner would need someone to look after the grounds?

"I'm devastated for Claudia and Tim," said Millie, indignation at their position fizzing in the pit of her stomach. "How will all this affect your position as estate manager?"

"The guy Dexter is bringing is apparently a wealthy Swedish internet entrepreneur who's publicity-phobic and wants to turn the manor into a fortress-like retreat, somewhere he can live in peace away from the media mayhem that surrounds him back home. Dexter has already sent photographs of the property and copies of the title deeds to Sven Andersen's lawyers and it sounds like it's a done deal. Thursday is just about the final recce. Tim was furious when Dexter told him that Sven plans to plant a twelve-foot-high leylandii hedge around the perimeter to prevent prying eyes and long lenses, but he was apoplectic when it was confirmed that he would not be retaining any of the staff."

"I'm sorry, Zach."

Millie's heart sunk to her toes as she watched Zach struggle to keep his emotions in check. This was a different side of Zach to the one she had encountered in St Lucia, the playful, good-humoured optimist who had filled her life with sparkle and her heart and soul with the confidence that she could do anything she put her mind to. Now it was her turn to step up and usher him down the positivity path, even if it meant she would lose him from her life.

"What are your options?"

"Tim's offered me a job in St Lucia if I want it. But Jake's happy there, for the moment at least, and I'm not sure they really need my services or whether they are just being kind."

"That's not the case at all! Once the hotel is up and running, you said yourself that Claudia intends to offer tours around the cocoa plantation – you know, 'From cocoa bean to chocolate chip dream'. You would make an amazing tour guide, Zach, and weren't you talking about organising quad bike safaris and archery shoots for the guests too? Not all the guests will want to spend the whole day cooking in the kitchen."

"Maybe…"

"So there'll be more than enough work to keep you *and* Jake busy."

The grandfather clock in the hallway struck midnight and Zach pushed back his chair to leave.

"Thanks for listening, Millie. You know, I really feel like I'm about to lose a treasured member of my family – an old maiden aunt who's being shipped off to a care home against her will, so heaven knows how Claudia is coping."

"You could look on it as an opportunity to start something new?" Millie suggested as she tossed the empty mugs into the sink and left them there for the morning.

She saw Zach's eyes linger briefly on the clutter; the fact that he chose not to comment, not even a chastisement, never mind a sarcastic response, worried her more than anything she had heard that night. She wanted to reassure him that everything would turn out fine, but she didn't see how that could happen and her hesitation gave Zach the signal to leave.

"Maybe. Look, I'd better go. We've both got an early start in the morning. Goodnight, Millie."

Zach paused at the boot room door for a few seconds, his mouth inches from hers. Goosebumps shot over her forearms at the sharp intensity of his gaze. All she wanted to do was fall into his arms and rekindle the closeness they had experienced during her sojourn at Claudia and Tim's spectacular villa high on the hill overlooking the bay of Soufrière, and when she scoured his eyes she saw that Zach felt the same.

However, just as Millie thought their lips were about to meet, Zach turned on his heels and left. Disappointment and confusion flooded her veins, but her overwhelming emotion was that of concern for what the director of Zach's destiny had in store for him. As she locked the door behind him and climbed the magnificent staircase to bed, her brain continued to churn over the details of their conversation until she was even more perplexed.

How did she feel about the possibility of Zach returning to St Lucia? If he did go, it would probably mean she would never see him again. But then their busy work schedules, coupled with her lingering fear of rejection, had conspired to keep them apart anyway. Nevertheless, it was still easier to dream of spending cosy weekends in the company of a gorgeous estate manager with a witty repertoire and a knack for making her feel like she could conquer the world when he was living in a cute little stone lodge in the Cotswolds rather than in a wooden cabin a ten-hour flight and a very bumpy taxi ride away!

Was that why he hadn't kissed her? Fear of starting something that couldn't be finished? But did that matter? She had definitely *wanted* him to kiss her. Maybe she *should* have taken Poppy's advice and carried an emergency sprig of mistletoe in her back pocket!

She undressed quickly and slid beneath the duvet, her thoughts chasing a myriad of possible solutions down blind alleyways, craving a lightbulb moment in which she could come up with a way to allow Zach to continue in the job he so clearly loved, and preferably closer to home.

Sleep came quickly again. It was so peaceful in the Hummingbird Suite; no sirens, no dogs barking, no crows bouncing on the TV aerials on the roof above her head, no late-night party goers shrieking their favourite rock ballads in the street below her attic window. She was well on her way down the chute towards slumber before she realised that the reason she was stretching her brain cells to come up with an answer to Zach's dilemma was because, despite the lack of a goodnight kiss, the emotions she was experiencing had progressed well beyond the bounds of friendship and into the less-well chartered waters of romance.

Chapter Seven

"Good morning everyone and a warm welcome to the Festive Feast cookery course at the Claudia Croft Cookery School. It's an early start so it's great to see you all so bright-eyed and raring to go!"

Gina laughed and nudged Leo who clearly looked as though he had just been dragged out of bed. His hair had ballooned into a halo of auburn curls that framed his ruggedly handsome features just like his namesake. He hadn't had chance to shave, and the smattering of golden stubble gave him an attractive, more relaxed look than the clean-shaven face he had presented when they had arrived the previous day. Gina had dressed for a day out on a Mediterranean yacht, her pixie-style crop immaculate just like her flared white trousers and Breton stripped tee shirt with the instantly recognisable designer logo on the sleeve. Unlike Leo, Gina was leaning across her workstation hanging on Claudia's every word.

"Okay, as you know, you are here to discover the variety of culinary delights on offer at Christmas. You will have seen from the itinerary that the week has been organised as a gastronomic journey through the various meals served on the most wonderful day of the year. So, today is all about preparing a sumptuous breakfast. Millie and I will demonstrate the recipes, coaching you where you need it, then we'll share the meal we have prepared, taking the opportunity to appraise each other's offerings."

"Marks out of ten?" asked Mike, pushing his glasses back up to the bridge of his nose and patting his quiff nervously.

"Mike, darling, it's not a competition! It's a tutorial," smiled Marianne who sported a scarlet cashmere jumper with sparkling silver snowflakes and the legend 'Let it Snow'.

"Well, thank God for that. You know how hopeless I am in the kitchen. I'd be the proud owner of five wooden spoons by the end of the week! So, Claudia, what do you have planned for us tomorrow?"

"A slightly later start, you'll be relieved to hear," she laughed. "We'll be focussing on a delicious brunch menu, which will lead us nicely to the main event on Wednesday – Christmas lunch with all the trimmings. On Thursday we'll be baking up a storm as we create an amazing High Tea, and then on Friday we'll make canapés and petit fours for an elegant evening soirée that will be the envy of your guests.

As Friday will be our last day together, I thought it might be nice to invite a few friends from the village to join us in celebration of what you have achieved, and to help us to eat all the products of your labours!"

"Sounds amazing!" exclaimed Marianne, clapping her hands in excitement, her eyes shining as she tied her pale lemon CC-logoed apron around her slender waist and positioned herself behind her workstation, ready to get started. "Mike, you're useless – you've got your apron on the wrong way round!"

There followed the best two hours Millie could remember in a kitchen. When she had worked with Luke in their restaurant in Oxford, every shift had been so full-on that she hadn't had time to appreciate the finer points of what she was creating. Then, at Étienne's patisserie, she was part of a team that worked together like a well-oiled machine producing the finest French pastries in Hammersmith - everyone in the room knew exactly what they were required to do so there was no need to discuss why the eggs had to be at room temperature, or the butter super-cold, or the flour sieved from a great height.

Chatting to Gina and Marianne, guiding them through the recipes by demonstrating and then assisting and explaining, was so rewarding that her self-confidence burgeoned until she was enjoying herself more than she had ever expected. She really hoped that the experience she had gained at the Paradise Cookery School, as well as here under the mentorship of the celebrated Claudia Croft, would stand her in good stead when she pursued her goal of becoming a presenter herself.

By ten thirty everything was ready and laid out on the huge marble table next to the French windows with cafetières of coffee, teapots of Earl Grey tea – as well as Marianne's favourite English Breakfast – set with a spectacular table decoration Claudia had fashioned from freshly harvested holly leaves, pine cones and wide gold ribbon. The four empty chairs had been removed, but Millie was a little saddened that their numbers were so depleted, especially as the roads had now been gritted – although the flat white expanse of snow on the manor's lawns remained undisturbed.

"So that's how you make the most fabulous breakfast with which to wow all your friends and family on Christmas morning!" smiled Millie, adding a sprinkle of fresh parsley to the platter of fragrant Kedgeree and setting it down on the table next to the basket of egg and smoked salmon cupcakes. The sweet aroma of warm buttery pastry pervaded every corner of the kitchen and her stomach rumbled in anticipation of sitting around the table with Claudia, Leo and Gina, and Mike and Marianne to sample the delights they had rustled up that morning.

Bright sunlight streamed through the French doors, washing the kitchen with a pale ivory glow and happiness spread through her veins. The group of avid foodies had turned out to be fascinating company, especially Leo who had regaled them with anecdotes from his daily life as a high-flying solicitor in the City specialising in matrimonial disputes for High Net Worth clients. What warring couples argued about amazed Millie. Why would anyone care enough about a silver cruet set to instruct a lawyer to correspond with their spouse's counterpart about it?

However, Millie felt more of an affinity with Marianne, not because she possessed a similar profusion of curls - hers the colour of burnished wheat, Marianne's the colour of a fox's tail - but because she was a cookery course addict. It turned out that she had attended over twenty tutorials in the last two years alone ranging from the sublime to the ridiculous – critter salad anyone?

"Oh, my God! I can't believe I made this!" exclaimed Gina, rolling her eyes in exaggerated ecstasy as she tasted the cranberry and cinnamon whirls she had created.

Her smile said it all, and the pleasure at accomplishing what was her first attempt at puff pastry was apparent. Even if Gina hadn't shared her occupation with the group before they had started their week-long culinary journey, Millie could have guessed that she was a member of the creative industry as her presentation of her savoury cupcakes was superb – just a shame about the non-artistically inspired burnt edges and the overzealous addition of a finely chopped red chilli. Leo had loyally declared that he loved them, only for his smile to turn to a frown as he reached for his coffee to douse the flames.

"I can't wait to get down to Cornwall and start preparing for the most fabulous Christmas ever!"

Whilst Leo had been concentrating on slicing his smoked salmon as thinly as possible, Gina had confided in Millie that her mother-in-law had never completely accepted the fact that her precious son had married a ballet dancer, hoping he would chose his partner from the ranks of his own profession. It hadn't helped that when they were first introduced Margaret Groves had thought her son had said his new girlfriend was a *belly* dancer and she had only been disabused of the fact when they had been invited to the theatre to see her perform, by which time the image had been stuck in her head for six months. Even now that they were married, whenever her mother-in-law visited them at their home in Kensington, she had taken every opportunity to question

Gina's choice of furnishings, the way she folded her laundry, not to mention how far down the culinary scale her supper offerings fell. But this year, Gina had declared that things were going to be different and Millie's heart blossomed at her enthusiasm.

"You know, if it was up to me we would just pile a load of ready-prepared food from Waitrose in the middle of the table and invite our guests to help themselves," laughed Leo. "That way everyone can eat whatever – and as much – as they like and no one would go hungry. It's such a waste of time and effort making all these magnificently intricate recipes to adorn the table! No offence Millie, but you wouldn't believe the stress levels last Christmas when we rented a cottage in the Lake District. Gina was so busy cooking in the kitchen, then making sure the table was perfect, that she hardly had any time to spend with our guests. Christmas is about the people you spend it with not about the food you devour! I know my mother is difficult to please, so why even try? She's a stubborn traditionalist – which is fine – but she can't understand that we want to create our own family traditions that might be different from hers – especially when we have a family of our own."

As he spoke the last words, Leo looked across the table at Gina with such adoration that Millie's heart performed a gymnastic tumble. Gina smiled back at him, raising her chin in a confident pose.

"Well, I now intend to channel my inner Claudia Croft to provide a sumptuous *traditional* feast which will be so outstanding in its excellence that everyone will declare me to be the new maestro on the culinary rostrum!"

"Don't take this the wrong way, darling, but my mother would find fault with the Queen's dining table!"

"I had the most fabulous mother-in-law," smiled Claudia, digging into her poached quail's eggs on home-made granary bread. "She was supportive of everything I tried to achieve. When I got my first publishing deal she threw the best party Hampshire had ever seen and invited every single one of her friends from the WI, even the local butcher, baker and upmarket candlemaker came along and she refused to allow them to leave before they had bought a book for me to sign. *The Baking Blend* was my first book and it's still my best seller, which I put down to Grace's own special brand of marketing and publicity skills."

Millie smiled as a warm blanket of contentment wrapped its corners around her shoulders while they enjoyed the products of their labours. Throughout the morning she had sent many glances in Claudia's direction, searching for the right moment to say something about the sale of the manor, but each time she got her on her own, Claudia excused herself and rushed off to assist Mike, the least accomplished of the foursome, before his cheese soufflé dissolved into mush.

It didn't take Millie long to get the hint that Claudia knew what was on her mind and was employing avoidance tactics. She was okay with that; after all, even though this would be the last Festive Feast course it was still Claudia's business and she had to maintain a professional approach even if her heart was cracking into tiny pieces. All she wanted to do was let Claudia know that she was there for her, to offer whatever help she could.

"Claudia? I have a favour to ask," said Leo as he scraped up the final grains of rice and swallowed down the last of his coffee, flashing a quick glance at Gina. "I know tomorrow is scheduled to feature a fabulous Christmas brunch, but do you think it would be possible to start the course after lunch? I'm sorry, there's a business deal I've been working on that I thought had gone off the boil, but it seems to have come back to life again. I need to make a couple of conference calls in the morning, and Gina and Marianne have a bit of Christmas shopping to do in Cheltenham."

"No problem at all," smiled Claudia, her crystal earrings shining like pole stars at her cheeks setting off her complexion perfectly. That morning, underneath her Claudia Croft Cookery School apron she wore a beautifully cut woollen drees in a gorgeous saffron colour that Millie knew had cost more than she earned in a month. "I have an idea. Why don't we move Thursday's demonstration of a Festive High Tea to tomorrow? That way it will be perfect timing to indulge in a spot of afternoon tea afterwards and we'll do the brunch on Thursday instead?"

"Oh, definitely! I love afternoon tea," squealed Marianne in delight. "My sister and I had the best Afternoon Tea at Fortum and Mason for my birthday in June. I'd love to learn how to make all those dainty French fancies."

"Well, you are in luck," smiled Claudia, flicking a smile in Millie's direction and causing her cheeks to colour. "Because Millie just happens to be an expert in French patisserie. So we'll make gourmet sandwiches, not a crust in sight, the best fig-and-walnut scones you will have ever tasted, and a selection of macarons, chocolate éclairs, strawberry fraisiers, and fresh fruit tarts."

"Mmm, my mouth is watering already!" laughed Mike, running his tongue over his lips in anticipation.

"Thanks for being flexible, Claudia. I'm sorry about messing up the schedule."

"It really isn't a problem. I'm sure Millie and I can find plenty of things to occupy ourselves in the morning."

"Yes, I did see Millie chatting to the most handsome man in Berryford last night," said Gina with a gleam in her eye. "Do we get an introduction?"

If Millie had coloured at Claudia's compliment earlier, this time she glowed with embarrassment. She jumped from her seat and made an attempt to collect the breakfast plates and slot them into the dishwasher. She could feel everyone's eyes scorching into the back of her head, so she took infinite care to load the crockery in the appropriate place, something she had never done before, preferring her usual haphazard approach to clearing up.

Claudia laughed. "I think you're referring to Zach Barker, Stonelea's estate manager. I'm sure he would be delighted to be invited to our soirée on Friday evening to sample our canapés, so you'll get to meet him then."

"Fabulous – this week just gets better and better!" laughed Gina, leaning forward to deposit a kiss on Leo's lips to indicate her true feelings. "Thanks for a great introduction to seasonal breakfasts, Claudia, Millie. I promise we'll be here for one o'clock sharp tomorrow, raring to go to learn how to bake the lightest scones this side of the M25. I can't wait because mine always seem to turn out like boulders, although I tell people they are actually rock cakes."

Millie watched their guests make their way back up the staircase and turned to smile at Claudia. "That went really well, didn't it?"

"Yes, thanks to you, Millie. But I have to admit, I'm exhausted so if you don't mind, I'm going to go for a lie down. Everything is sorted for tomorrow so why don't you have the rest of the day to yourself? Do you know what you might like to do?"

"Oh, I thought I'd choose a book and curl up on one of the window seats in the library."

"Well, if you don't mind, would you be able to help me out and deliver this package to Zach's lodge? I really don't have the energy to get bundled up in a hat, scarf and gloves, not to mention a pair of Wellington boots, and go trotting down the driveway. I think I'll feel better after a snooze."

"No problem."

Millie smiled, but concern for her friend swirled through her chest. However, a small part of her did wonder whether Claudia was really exhausted, which seemed unlikely as she was a seasoned presenter and they had only spent three hours in the kitchen, or whether she was intent on giving her potential relationship with Zach a helping hand.

She took the parcel, gave Claudia a hug, and strode to the boot room. She surveyed her choices and selected a fleece-lined wax jacket and a woolly hat with cute mouse ears and a pink nose and whiskers sewn onto the brim, and set off down the driveway towards the entrance gate. It was just after midday and the sun was trying its best to wriggle through the grey clouds. There was a nip in the air – it wasn't as cold as when she had arrived but not warm enough to melt the snow on the lawn.

She pushed open the tiny wooden gate to Zach's lodge and a huge smile stretched her lips at the sound of excited barking coming from behind the pale green door.

Binks!

She should have been prepared for the bundle of black-and-white fur to launch a frenzied welcome, but she wasn't, and ended up on her bottom as the springer spaniel whom she had met in St Lucia welcomed her to his home.

"Hi Binks! It's great to see you, too, but do you think you could just let me get up – it's bit cold on the buttocks down here!"

Binks gave her an affectionate lick and trotted back to his master's side, his pink tongue hanging from a wide grin.

"Hey, Millie. For a girl who professes to hate the snow you do seem to spend an inordinate amount of time rolling in the stuff!" smirked Zach, his eyes twinkling as he offered her his hand to drag her upright.

A surge of relief whipped through Millie at the re-emergence of the upbeat animation that had always been a permanent fixture in Zach's demeanour: Zach being cheeky about her foibles - the world was turning normally; Zach being downbeat and introspective - very disturbing indeed. His sarcasm had irritated her when she had first encountered him in St Lucia – sadly whilst rolling around in a puddle - but she had grown to enjoy their verbal sparring, to appreciate the way he challenged her to look at life from a different perspective, to seek out new adventures, to squeeze every last crumb of pleasure from every situation. She knew that if she hadn't met Zach, she would still be wallowing under a cloud of misery at the way Luke had dumped her, instead of viewing it as a blip on life's rocky highway.

"To what do Binks and I owe the honour of your visit?"

"Oh, yes, sorry. Claudia ask me to deliver this," she said, handing over the package.

"Thanks. So, how did the first day of the fabulous Festive Feast course go?"

"It went really well, plus I've just indulged in a breakfast fit for a very hungry giant! Tomorrow's itinerary has changed though. We're doing our Christmas-themed afternoon tea that had been scheduled for Thursday. I'll save you a few turkey and cranberry sandwiches if you promise not to critique the symmetry of my bread-cutting skills!"

"Now why would I do that?"

Zach met her gaze and smiled, sending her stomach into a maelstrom of confusion. She had been with Luke for two years and she could honestly say, hand on heart, that she had never experienced such a vivid reaction when he'd looked at her. In fact, the strongest reaction he'd instilled in her had been one of devastation, followed by a long, slow burn of mortification. She belatedly realised that Zach was scouring her expression, as if watching the mini film reel flicker behind her eyes, his lips turned upwards to reveal the cute dimples that bracketed his mouth and she felt heat seep into her cheeks.

"So, if you've finished your duties for the day, I've got an idea. Come on."

Millie laughed as he grabbed her hand and dragged her across the pristine expanse of the manor's lawn at the rear of his lodge, their footsteps creating an ad hoc pattern in the undisturbed snow. Binks bounded in their wake, joining in the fun, bouncing and barking with abandon.

"Do you want to build a snowman?" asked Millie, quoting her nieces' Lily and Sofia's best-loved phrase, except Zach took her literally.

"Yes! A girl after my own heart. Let's make it interesting though and have a competition. Points for the best twist on the theme. Ready, steady, go!"

And before she could remind Zach that snow was her most hated weather element, he had zipped away to make a start on rolling a huge boulder of snow. She sighed and began to build a mound which she thought looked like a passable imitation of Binks with a pebble for his nose and a waggy tail made from twig. She was no Henry Moore, but at least she'd had a go – and it was the very first snow sculpture she had ever assembled.

When she looked around to compare her effort with Zach's he was nowhere to be seen, until she noticed the top of his red bobble hat poking above the parapet of the stone wall that encircled the lodge's back garden.

Why had he decided to build his snowman there? Was it because his masterpiece was so much better than hers, or because at last she had stumbled on something he was terrible at? She suspected it was the former, but before she could go and find out, Zach was jogging towards her to scrutinise her own work of art.

"What's that? A seal?"

"No! It doesn't look anything like a seal!"

"Sorry, a mermaid? A unicorn?"

"No! It's Binks!"

"Sorry, mate."

Zach tossed a sympathetic glance at Binks who was sitting with his head on one side, contemplating his likeness like a seasoned art critic. The look he gave his master made Millie giggle. She had to acknowledge that she had a lot to learn when it came to ice sculpture.

"Come on then, let's see yours!"

She had taken only a few steps towards the lodge when a snowball flew through the air and landed with a splat on the top of her head, sending a cascade of snow down the collar of her coat.

"Hey!"

She turned to look at Zach, her eyes wide with surprise. Not being a fan of the snow, she had studiously avoided any encounter with the white stuff throughout her childhood. Therefore, she had never engaged in a snowball fight, and still cringed when she saw the game played out between Lily and Sofia from the warmth – and safety – of the conservatory at her sister's home in Hampshire.

However, as she watched Zach reach down again to gather more ammunition, giving her a very pleasant view of his toned buttocks, a surge of determination blasted through her veins. Zach had encouraged her to discard her comfort blanket whilst they were in St Lucia and she'd had the most fun of her life by flying through the treetops on a zip wire. This time the challenge was different – and, of course, much colder – but no less exhilarating. She crouched down to gather a snowball of her own and ran towards Zach, her arm raised ready to pitch the icy missile, but at last minute her toe connected with a hidden obstacle and she fell flat on her face at his feet.

Zach roared with laughter, wisps of mist from his warm breath lingering in the air. "You never cease to amaze me with your capacity for calamity, Millie!"

Millie rolled over onto her back and flapped her arms and legs to make a snow angel, something she had seen Lily and Sofia do.

"What's the matter? Scared you'll get a speck of dirt on that pristine jacket of yours?"

"No. Why?"

Zach lay down next to her to make his own snow angel and Millie took the opportunity to sling a huge dollop of snow in his face.

"Take that!"

But within seconds she received similar treatment and found herself pinned down in the snow, Zach holding her wrists and staring down into her eyes, scouring her soul. She was suddenly scared of what he might see lurking there, so she averted her gaze, only to have Binks lick the snow from her face.

"Euew!"

The moment passed and Zach scrambled to his feet, helping her upright.

"Fancy thawing out with a mug of the best hot chocolate the Cotswolds has to offer?"

"Sounds like paradise!" she laughed, suddenly keen to see the inside of the lodge that Zach called home.

However, much to Millie's disappointment, Zach didn't steer her towards his front door, but to the passenger seat of his Golf.

"Hop in!"

Chapter Eight

"Where are we going?"

"Into Berryford."

"For the best hot chocolate in the world?"

"Well, in Gloucestershire – yes."

"Okay."

Millie settled into her seat and dragged off her hat, patting down her wayward curls. She glanced across at Zach, his eyes fixed on the road ahead, his hands strong and sure on the steering wheel and tufts of dark hair standing to attention after being freed from the confines of his beanie.

Her heart ballooned and she experienced the familiar feeling of exhilaration that always bubbled to the surface whenever she was in Zach's company. If anyone had asked her as she got ready for her engagement party eight months ago, with her best friend Frankie making a great job of plaiting her hair into an elegant chignon, she would have insisted that she had no qualms in trusting her future happiness to Luke, that she loved him and that was all that mattered.

But Luke had never made her feel such heights of emotions; depths, yes, when he had abandoned her at the hotel ballroom they had hired and left her to explain to both sets of relatives and all their friends why he wasn't at the party.

It had been the most confidence-draining event of her life, but even she hadn't suspected that there was worse to come when she eventually discovered the identity of the woman he'd ditched her for. Okay, her identity had no bearing on how hurt she was, she would have been devastated no matter who he had chosen instead of her. She had been shocked to the core, but not as mortified as Frankie had been to discover that Luke had decided to spend his life with her mother instead of her best friend. TS Eliot had been right, April was the cruellest month!

None of that was Frankie's fault. Millie hadn't blamed her for what had happened, yet it had been the end of their friendship because two weeks later Millie had hightailed it to London and she hadn't been back to Oxford since.

In that moment, as Zach steered into a parking spot outside the village café, she realised she missed Frankie and her cheerful take on life, that the void in her heart she had thought was Luke-shaped was in fact where Frankie had been. She resolved to pay her a visit as soon as the Festive Feast cookery course had concluded, armed with an abundance of Christmas cheer and goodies. Why should she allow Luke to take her best friend from her along with everything else he stole on that fateful day in early April? It wouldn't be easy - nothing worthwhile was ever easy – especially after she had seen on a mutual friend's Facebook page that Luke and Donna were expecting a baby in January which meant Frankie would have a half-sibling.

She'd had trouble processing that piece of information, and whenever she had tried to give it some thought, her emotions morphed into a haphazard mess. She hadn't even shared the news with Poppy, but maybe a chat with a friend who had known her inside and out from the age of ten would help her work it through and perhaps at the same time she could return the favour. She had no idea how Frankie felt about having a sibling twenty-five years younger than she was. Not only was it a huge age-gap, but Frankie had always been very close to her mother who had given birth to her at the tender age of seventeen. Millie recalled many occasions when mother and daughter had been mistaken for sisters, much to Donna's delight and Frankie's cheerful disgust.

"Earth to Millie?"

"Oh, sorry."

"Everything okay?"

"Fine. Fine. So this is where they make the best hot chocolate, is it?"

"Yes, come on."

Millie jumped from the passenger seat and followed Zach towards the quaint little teashop. It was the first time she had seen Berryford in the daylight and the village was Christmas card perfect. Shafts of welcome sunshine wriggled through the clouds highlighting the buildings with a copper-infused radiance, their roofs finished off with a dribble of white icing. Of course, the magnificent Christmas tree had become the focal point of the village green, with the village hall on one side, The Flying Fox pub on the other, and a row of cottages built from the same honeyed stone as Stonelea Manor to their left.

"It's so pretty, isn't it?" she sighed. "The way the snow sits on the branches and along the eaves of the church."

"Are my ears deceiving me? Can it be that Amelia Harper, advocate of tropical breeze, palm trees and sun-drenched beaches is submitting to the jury a soliloquy on the positives of the snow-covered English countryside?"

"Maybe," she laughed as she caught her first glimpse of Kate's Kitchen.

A plethora of twinkling fairy lights laced the bow-fronted windows of the café like a giant's necklace and the jolly beat of *I Wish It Could Be Christmas Every Day* spilled out into the street. It was impossible to see inside as an opaque sheet of condensation masked the windows, with streamers of water running down to the sill. When Zach pushed opened the door, the tinkle of the brass bell made her smile which turned into a full-on beam when she saw who was rushing forward to greet her.

"Millie, darling! You came!"

"Hello, Blake. I'm reliably informed that you make the best hot chocolate in the whole of the county, so no pressure."

"Your sources are as immaculate as your taste in companions," Blake smirked, sending Zach a mischievous wink. "Grab a seat and I'll be right over."

Millie chose a table next to the window, peeled off her borrowed wax jacket and took a moment to glance around the room. Kate's Kitchen was like any traditional café you'd stumble across in many of the villages peppered around the Cotswolds. She knew a few enterprising owners had traded up to become chic bistros, offering a diverse range of organic, locally-sourced menus; pheasant, rabbit, goose accompanied by fresh asparagus and samphire and home-made ginger and melon ice cream.

However, it was apparent that the eponymous Kate had chosen not to follow this dash into the

'Elite Culinary Club' to satisfy her customers. The interior presented a neat synopsis of village life; warm, welcoming and relaxed. Every corner had been decorated with handmade wreaths of holly and ivy jostling for space against their more brazen cousins – wire rings woven with neon-coloured tinsel and baubles. The whole ensemble was presided over by a Christmas tree that would not have looked out of place in Barbie's weekend castle. Who knew you could even *buy* cerise-pink tinsel Christmas trees?

Animated chatter swirled around the room on the wings of the most delicious fragrance of warm spices mingled with vanilla and honey and the strange addition of a top-note of chlorine. She glanced at the young couple at the lemon gingham-covered table next them, ploughing their way through a sharing platter crammed with doorstopper sandwiches, triangles of home-baked corned-beef-and-potato pie and a short pyramid of well-risen cheese scones. On a rosebud patterned china cake-stand were slabs of cake and a selection of miniature jam doughnuts.

Millie thought of the afternoon tea they served at Étienne's; thinly sliced cucumber or smoked salmon and cream cheese sandwiches, melt-in-your-mouth fruit scones with lashings of Chantilly cream and homemade raspberry jam, and a selection of dainty patisseries to round off the treat, all beautifully presented on Etiènne's signature gold-rimmed Royal Doulton china. It would look like a doll's tea party compared to this hearty fayre. She hoped that Blake wasn't thinking of bringing them one to sample. She didn't think her stomach could cope after the over-indulgence of breakfast.

"Oh, don't mind them," scoffed Blake, catching her staring at her neighbours and misinterpreting her frown as one of disapproval for their canoodling. With a flourish worthy of a music maestro he deposited two tall mugs, topped with swirls of cream and crowned with flakes of chocolate, on the table in front of them. "Grant and Martha got together at the tree lighting party last night and they're already acting like the new Harry and Meghan. Ooops, forgive me, I forgot to bring your cake!"

Blake rushed back to the counter, his gingham apron flapping at his waist, and carefully carried two china places back to their table as though they were the crown jewels.

"Voilà!"

"What exactly *is* this?" asked Millie, wrinkling her nose as she eyed the slab of treacle-laced cake. She could almost feel her arteries contracting in horror as she contemplated a taste-test. Up close, the cake looked more like something she would use to build a barbeque than enjoy as an afternoon treat.

"Try it."

Millie broke off a corner and was surprised at how heavy and dense it was. Give her a glazed fruit tart or a raspberry and vanilla crème mille-feuille and she'd been the happiest pastry chef in the Cotswolds. She had never been a fan of lard-based pastry, or of heavy suet puddings, or jam donuts either.

"Well, I'd love to stay and chat, but my customers need me! Enjoy!"

"What's the matter?" asked Zach, noticing her hesitation and a glint of familiar mischief appearing in his mahogany eyes. "Ah, is Kate's baking not up to your Parisian Patisserie School standards?"

"No, it's not that at all." Millie gaped, horrified that his suggestion may have been overheard. It made her sound like an elitist foodie snob. She indulged in another sip of the hot chocolate, a little too sweet for her taste but still delicious, wrapping her fingers around the handle and hugging the glass cup to her chest.

"What then?" he persisted.

"It's just," she glanced over her shoulder and lowered her voice, "it's all a little stodgy, don't you think? More what you'd feed a trucker at a roadside greasy spoon than a discerning tourist visiting one of England's most picturesque counties."

Zach chuckled as he crammed a piece of the rejected parkin into his mouth, licking his lips with exaggerated relish. "I grew up eating good wholesome baking like this."

"Well, that certainly explains a lot."

Zach ignored her retort. "The majority of Kate's customers are hikers, cyclists and ramblers – people who spend their day yomping around this glorious countryside, equipped with only a rucksack and a walker's pole for company. They need good hearty food to keep their energy levels up. What use is a pistachio-infused macaron, or a profiterole filled with crème pâtissière and dribbled with cucumber juice, going to be? They'd keel over like a bunch of maiden aunts overcome by a bout of the vapours. Extreme cyclists love savoury dumplings floating in rich casseroles, long-distance hikers adore toasted crumpets dripping with butter. Anyway, what else is a Croque-Monsieur but a cheese and ham toastie?"

Millie took a tentative bite of the parkin and experienced a sharp slap to her taste buds causing her to grimace. She briefly wondered whether Zach and Blake had set her up so that they could tease her about her baking snootiness. She narrowed her eyes as Zach continued with his culinary caper, watched over by a smirking Blake from the counter.

"Kate's parkin is made from an old family recipe. I'm sure she wouldn't mind sharing it with you if you were thinking of introducing it at the patisserie paradise you work in in Hammersmith? Maybe it's exactly what your customers have been craving all these years."

"I very much doubt it. Étienne's serve only the freshest, locally-sourced fruits with our desserts, not this suet-filled, artery-clogging...."

"Ah, Kate, can I introduce you to Amelia Harper?"

Chapter Nine

Heat flooded Millie's face as she calculated whether Kate had heard her prognosis on her country fayre. She watched in horror as Zach stood up from his seat and bent down to deposit a kiss on the teashop owner's cheek before stage whispering in her ear "Don't mind Millie - she's French and prefers to indulge in those dainty little mince pies and chocolate roulades we had at the party last night - perfect if you're planning an afternoon tea with Barbie's pet unicorn. Ooops, sorry, sorry," he held up his palm in Millie's direction, tossing her a mischievous look, "*half* French."

"Which half? Top or bottom?" asked Blake, his bright blue eyes glinting as he re-joined their conversation and made Millie feel even worse.

She ignored Zach and Blake's amusement and plastered on her brightest smile. "Hello, Kate. It's lovely to meet you. I'm helping Claudia present the Festive Feast cookery course at Stonelea Manor this week."

"Yes, Claudia mentioned that Tim had persuaded her to ask for some help. I have to admit I'm worried about her. She's always been so efficient and capable, running those workshops of hers with boundless energy. That riding accident in September seems to have knocked the stuffing out of her, though, never mind being laid up with her leg in plaster for six weeks. I hope she's taking it easy?"

Kate raised her eyebrows, giving Millie the impression that she thought it was her personal responsibility to protect Claudia's wellbeing by doing all the hard work herself. Her dark hazel eyes then narrowed, and Millie felt as though her deepest thoughts had been scoured with a wire brush. Her non-too-subtle hint delivered, Kate's face morphed into a smile, stretching her perfectly applied scarlet lipstick. Before Millie could respond, Kate had drifted away to chat to the couple at the next table, patting her freshly-set auburn waves that had been moulded into something akin to a Russian Cossack's fur hat and leaving behind an aroma of lily-of-the-valley and caramel.

"Oh my God, do you think she heard what I said about her cooking?"

"About it being 'stodgy and artery-clogging' and the sole reason our generation is prone to frequent heart attacks and strokes?" asked Blake, eyeing Millie's uneaten parkin and giving her a cheeky grin as he confirmed helpfully, "Probably."

"Oh no. I have to go and apologise."

Millie began to push herself out of her chair, but Zach pressed his fingers to her forearm. "No need. It was an honest critique, and Kate's no shrinking violet. It'd take more than a passing stranger's opinion on the heaviness of her pastry to upset her."

Millie was shocked to experience a sharp stab of discomfort at being described by Zach as a mere 'passing stranger'. Of course, it was an accurate description as far as her acquaintance with Kate was concerned and he was probably just trying to make her feel better about her totally unnecessary rudeness, yet she found she suddenly wanted to be a part of this tight-knit community. She had only been in Berryford for three days and she already felt like she belonged there. Ridiculous, she knew.

"Come on, I'll drive you back to the manor before you cause any more trouble," smirked Zach. "Claudia will be thinking I've kidnapped you!"

Millie watched Zach settle their bill at the counter, sharing a joke with Blake before again pecking Kate on the cheek. Did every customer of Kate's Kitchen do that when they left? A surge of envy rolled through her stomach, swiftly followed by relief. There was no way she would want to embrace the customers of

Étienne's, if for no other reason than she would be at it all day!

However, there was something so heart-warming about the way everyone knew everyone else and looked out for each other's wellbeing – just as Kate had done with Claudia – instilling a sense that whatever happened, Claudia and Tim were not alone, that the villagers would be there to support them in good times and in bad. No wonder Claudia was so distressed about the sale of the manor - not for selfish reasons but because of the impact its change of ownership would inevitably have on the community. She assumed that was why there had been such a lacklustre attempt at filling the house with cheery Christmas decorations; they simply hadn't been able to face it.

Whilst Zach navigated the bends in the road back to Stonelea, Millie took the opportunity to survey the landscape, still dressed in its winter clothing. Once again, she experienced that special feeling of belonging, of the warm welcome she had received from everyone despite being a 'passing stranger'. She knew she wanted to be more than that, she wanted to become an integral part of the village life, but of course it was too late. Claudia and Tim were relocating to St Lucia and, unless he took them up on their offer to go with them, Zach would be out of a job and a home, and who knew where he would end up living - and she suspected that Kate wouldn't be bothered if she never set eyes on her again.

"Okay, here we are," announced Zach as he pulled into the cobbled courtyard at the rear of the manor. "Erm, Millie, would you like to come for dinner tomorrow night? I'll cook — that's if you have room after scoffing all the goodies on the menu at the Christmas High Tea?"

She turned in her seat to face Zach. His invitation, and the look of hopefulness reflected in his eyes, was a welcome confirmation that, despite his earlier attempts at keeping their relationship firmly on the friendship rung, his feelings for her had also moved up a level. Her heart performed a somersault of pleasure and she could think of nothing else she would rather do than spend more time in his company, this time in the more intimate surroundings of his home, with a bottle of Chianti breathing on the coffee table, Binks snoozing at their feet and a fire burning in the grate.

"Yes please! What about one of those amazing Spag Bols you made in St Lucia?"

"You're on!" he smiled.

"Great. See you tomorrow, then."

Millie slammed the passenger door shut and watched Zach perform an elaborate a three-point turn before trundling off back down the driveway to his lodge. When he was out of sight, she stuck her hands in her pockets, raised her shoulders towards her ears and performed a perfect pirouette of delight.

The sharp ring of a hammer on iron interrupted her spontaneous celebration of Zach's surprise dinner invitation and she decided to investigate what was going on in one of the old outhouses on the other side of the courtyard. Her spirits climbed another notch when a stream of choice profanities met her ears. She had stumbled on Tim's workshop!

She approached the scarred wooden door with caution, unsure of her welcome, not to mention her safety after hearing Claudia's numerous anecdotes about her husband's penchant for blowing thing up – the last being an old washing machine he was trying to turn into a battery-powered go-kart.

"Tim? It's Millie. Is it okay to come in?"

"Oh, hi Millie. Yes, fine. Just be careful of the bench saw over there, it's still switched on. Oh, and you might like to avoid the Bunsen burner with that scarf dangling round your neck."

Millie lingered for a few moments on the threshold, allowing her eyes to adjust to the gloom and when they did, her jaw dropped. The whole place looked like a batty old scientist's Aladdin's cave, in the middle of which stood the batty old scientist himself. Tim's thick hair stood on end and he looked like he'd just electrocuted himself – a not inconceivable possibility, but more likely due to the fact he'd been running his fingers through his fringe in frustration. Smudges of engine oil were streaked across his cheeks like war paint – except the bulky navy-blue boiler suit, covered in splodges of plaster, made him look more like a benign, if scruffy, cousin of the Teletubbies.

He stood with a wrench in his hand staring at an upside-down, ride-on lawn mower, glaring at it as though it were the enemy and all he wanted to do was bash it into submission but he was just too polite to do so.

"I just don't seem to be able to turn that final corner, Millie," he mused as if she had any inkling of what he was talking about. "Any ideas?"

A blast of mirth spluttered from Millie's throat at the most unexpected question she had ever been asked. Tim must have realised what he had said and smiled at her. "Sorry."

"This is a fantastic workshop, Tim."

"It's a palace, don't care what Claudia calls it. She's refused to set foot in here for over a year now, but I must admit I don't blame her. Before she left me to my own devices though, she gave me a very boring lecture on the numerous Health and Safety rules the council Gestapos insist on for the cookery school. She made me promise to sort out a sturdy padlock and as long as I remember to lock up at the end of the day, I should be okay."

"So what exactly are you working on?" asked Millie, taking a few steps towards the machine whose wheels were spinning in the air like an up-ended tortoise.

Tim's eyes lit up at her interest and her heart softened towards him. If she ever had the space, this was exactly the kind of sanctuary she wanted, albeit a little cleaner and filled to the rafters with culinary paraphernalia rather than rust-blistered old tools, myriad jars of nails and screws, and every electronic gadget a DIY enthusiast could ever dream of owning. She glanced upwards and took another speedy stride inside when she saw an old-fashioned scythe dangling above her head secured with only a tatty length of rope.

"This, Millie, is a sit-on lawn mower, but it's no ordinary sit-on lawn mower. One day, this machine will mow the lawns here at Stonelea by remote control – you know, like a cross between those robotic vacuum cleaners and a driverless car. I just need to iron out a few teething problems and then.... Oh, sorry, I recognise that glazed look. I can get a little over-zealous when it comes to engineering projects."

"It's okay."

Millie spotted a tattered old cardboard box abandoned on a tool-strewn workbench and went over to investigate. She rooted around inside and removed a beautifully illustrated piece of parchment. It was a hand-written recipe for a Christmas cake complete with drawings of the ingredients in the margins and a photograph of the final triumph at the bottom. It was a work of art which should have been framed and hung on the wall in the kitchen, not lurking in a damp decrepit box where the slightest lapse could send the place up in flames.

"Why are these recipe cards here?"

"Ah, yes, thank you for reminding me, Millie. I'd completely forgotten. I have to make sure that I get them FedExed to Claudia's agent, Giles Morton, in tonight's post otherwise I'll go straight to the top of Claudia's naughty list."

"Some of these are beautiful. Look at this white chocolate cheesecake recipe! It's got honey and whiskey in it – now that's my kind of cheesecake. Oh, and this one for a Christmas pithivier. I add apricots and passion fruit to the mincemeat when I make mine, but Mum does hers with plums and cherries and a splash of vodka which is absolutely delicious. The illustrations are amazing."

"They're the winning recipes the cookery school has showcased from each of the last ten years. Forty in total – all traditional bakes that the villagers rustled up for their families at Christmas. Claudie commissioned a local artist to sketch the ingredients and the finished products from the photographs of the students' attempts. Her agent saw them when he was on a visit down here when Claudie was laid up after her riding accident and adored them. Giles took a selection back to London with him and he reckons he might have a publisher interested. The meeting is tomorrow, and I really should have sent them on Saturday, but never got round to it. It might be best if you didn't mention that slip-up to Claudie. I'll call Giles and tell him they'll be with him in the morning."

Tim grimaced at the inconvenience, dropping his wrench onto a bench where it joined several identical friends - as well as an assortment of spanners and a cascade of nuts and bolts - with a resounding clatter. Millie rolled her eyes – and Zach thought *she* had a problem with the clutter gene! He grabbed the box, closed the lid, and deposited it in the doorway so that he would have to trip over it when he left.

"Oooo, what's this you're working on?"

"Ah, yes, it's rather nice, isn't it? It's a piece of stained glass I've designed for Claudie's Christmas present."

"Is that the view of the Pitons from the villa?"

"Yes, it is. I'd forgotten you've been there. Thank you, Millie. You've done a great deal for us over the last couple of months. It's a shame the manor is being sold, otherwise I think Claudie would have offered you a position here."

Millie's eyes widened with delight and her heart filled with gratitude until she remembered that it was a purely hypothetical career opportunity.

"Wow, that would be my dream job!"

"Well, you can join the queue to punch Dexter's lights out when he shows his face on Thursday. You won't be surprised to hear that yours are not the only dreams he's trampled on. I'm sure you're aware how upset Claudie is about what's happened. But she refuses to talk about it and I know it's at the root of her current fatigue. She's always been the life and soul of everything she sets her mind to and I hate seeing her so downhearted."

Tim stopped fiddling with one of the wheels on the lawn mower, shoved his fingers through his hair then ran his palm over his chin.

"The problem is, she loves her cousin. They spent a carefree childhood together here at Stonelea, running around the grounds like a pair of kids from Swallows and Amazons or the Famous Five or something. She wants to be angry with him, but she can't so she's just bottling up her emotions and it's not good. I know Dexter is only asking for what's rightfully his *and* that he's waited over ten years for it, but if he had just given us more notice maybe we could have come up with the cash."

Tim's eyes reflected the ragged pain that was swirling around his heart. "Dexter has always been irresponsible and impulsive in everything he does, so it's no surprise he's carried that trait through to his business dealings and investment decisions. Sometimes that works to his advantage; sometimes it's disastrous. I have no idea what possessed him to choose a start-up mining company in the Australian outback to sink his cash into, but I've told Claudie we have to be pragmatic. We have a fabulous project to get our teeth into in St Lucia. She has lots of plans, as you know, and as soon as we get over there in January I'm sure a dose of sunshine therapy will do wonders to raise her spirits. I hope so after the year we've had."

Millie saw Tim flick a glance in her direction from beneath his lashes and knew that there was something else apart from the problems with Stonelea Manor that he wasn't telling her. Something much more personal that upset him even more than the loss of his home. She wondered what it could be, but she didn't want to pry. It was just another mystery to add to the list. If he had wanted her to know he would have told her, but her heart squeezed with sadness for the challenges they both faced.

Tim had turned his back on her and sunk into silence, clearly battling his demons as he fiddled with the plug of a circular saw. She decided to press a little more on the subject of Claudia's cousin's imminent arrival in the hope she could find a way of helping, even if it was in a small way.

"So, Dexter is coming on Thursday? Does he know that our Festive Feast guests are still going to be here?"

"Claudie tried to put him off, but he's bringing the guy who wants to buy the manor with him because that's the only day in his 'very busy schedule' that he can squeeze in a trip to look around." A flicker of irritation stalked across Tim's expression. "He's apparently some kind of Swedish entrepreneur. You know the type: young, wealthy, a privacy-obsessed internet celebrity, which is complete oxymoron if you ask me! Never heard of him, of course, but he wants to turn Stonelea into a sort of retreat from the prying eyes of his adoring public. Wants to dig out the foundations to make a gym and leisure complex! What I really object to, though, are his plans to erect a three-metre-high fence around the perimeter of the estate. Sven Andersen doesn't sound like the kind of guy who's going to welcome the interference of the local community, or get involved in anything himself, and that's what's upsetting Claudie."

Tim wiped his forehead with the back of his hand leaving a trial of soot. The temperature in the workshop had been getting progressively higher as they had been talking and Millie could feel perspiration tingling at her temples and beneath her breasts. It was time to leave Tim to his experiments.

"I'm really sorry about the house, Tim. If there's anything at all I can do to help..."

Despite being keen to make her excuses and escape, she thought she had better mention the acidic stench of scorched metal that was invading her nostrils and scorching the back of her throat.

"Erm, Tim?"

"Mmm?" muttered Tim distractedly as he leaned down to retrieve his wrench and consider his next move in the invention of the century.

"What's that smell?"

"What smell...? Oh, Jesus!"

In a flash, Tim whipped the fire extinguisher from its hook and blasted the rear wall of the workshop with a blanket of foam before reaching for what looked to Millie like a long wooden stick with a rubber end to cut the electricity supply. However, by removing the stick so carelessly, Tim managed to dislodge another of his weird contraptions which tumbled down from the rafters, jettisoning a protruding plank of wood into the roof, which in turn dislodged several terracotta tiles that fell to the floor and smashed to smithereens.

"Oh my God!" squealed Millie, cowering as she watched the events unfold through splayed fingers. She felt as though she was in the audience of a particularly realistic stage farce where she knew the main protagonist was about to blow the place up.

"Don't panic, everything's under control!" said Tim calmly as if that sort of thing happened every day.

It probably did happen every day, thought Millie as she tried to make her getaway only to trip over the cardboard box Tim had discarded in the doorway. Claudia was right. Ten minutes in Tim's company and you had to take your life in your hands!

Chapter Ten

On Tuesday morning, Millie spent a leisurely extra hour in bed, hugging a cup of coffee and leafing through one of Claudia's cookery books, drooling over the recipes and the glossy photographs that accompanied them. She had carried up a selection from the library the previous evening and had fallen asleep with her favourite - *The Baking Blend* - hugged to her chest like a treasured teddy bear. How wonderful it must be to have your own cookery book published, thought Millie, never mind twenty!

She glanced around her suite, so tropical and bright, but the ambience was spoiled by the bibliographic paraphernalia scattered around the floor. So much for her resolution to reign in her untidy tenancies. Poppy would be disappointed. She leapt out of bed, gathered up the cookery books and piled them neatly on her bedside table. Next, she scooped up her discarded clothes and hung them in the wardrobe before collecting her toiletries and lining them up, Zach-style, along the glass shelf in the bathroom.

Better, she sighed, contemplating taking a quick snap to send to Poppy to prove to her that she was a reformed character. But her friend deserved more than a swift text and she resolved to call her that night before she went to sleep.

After a refreshing shower, she grabbed a short tartan skirt, black roll-necked sweater and woolly tights, and slotted her toes into a pair of Gucci-style flats. She fluffed up her curls and, with minimum attention to makeup, galloped along the corridor to the top of the stairs where she paused, a crazy thought running through her mind.

Could she? She knew Leo and Mike would be sequestered in the library on their business calls and she had seen Gina and Marianne drive away in Leo's Mercedes for the highly anticipated Christmas shopping trip to Cheltenham over an hour ago. It was the perfect opportunity to indulge in a childhood fantasy.

She took a quick glance over her shoulder to see if anyone was lurking in the shadows of the split gallery landing, then cocked her leg over the banister. She was about to let go when she recalled Claudia's story about Dexter breaking his wrists whilst doing precisely what she intended to do. But the tickertape of trepidation was interrupted by Zach's voice urging her to go for it, to try everything once and see where it took her, so she gritted her teeth and let go. The sense of exhilaration as she slid all the way to the bottom was huge, despite landing in an undignified heap on the parquet flooring.

As she picked herself up, triumph whipping through her chest, Zach's laughing face floated across her vision. Her newly acquired adventurous streak was purely down to his encouragement, whether it be zip-lining through the rainforest, riding on the back of a snow mobile, or learning how to move on from heartbreak and contemplate the possibility of falling in love again – as scary as that had once seemed after the debacle with Luke.

She filed away that last possibility for later contemplation because she and Claudia had a jam-packed morning of culinary preparation to do for that afternoon's tutorial on creating the most sumptuous Christmassy-themed afternoon tea. She had just set the kettle to boil and scooped a generous measure of freshly ground coffee into the cafetière when Claudia arrived in the kitchen, one of her signature scarves tied around her neck, this one screaming the colours of the St Lucian flag; sunshine yellow, cerulean blue and black.

"Morning, Millie. Did you sleep well?"

"Better than ever, thanks. I really wish I could wrap up the Hummingbird Suite and take it home with me to London. I feel so relaxed here. Stonelea Manor is an amazing place."

"Thanks, darling."

Claudia turned away from Millie on the pretext of collecting a freshly laundered apron, but Millie knew her emotions had got the better of her friend again.

"Claudia…"

"Sorry, don't mind me. I'm fine. Nothing a session in the kitchen won't cure. Come on, let's get cracking!"

Millie spent the next two hours responding to Claudia's directions, and storing away every nugget of advice for future reference in case her dream of becoming a cookery course presenter came true. She chopped, sliced, peeled and weighed out six separate sets of the ingredients they would need to prepare the Cotswolds Cookery School's take on a festive High Tea. Bowls of sliced cucumber, egg mayonnaise with a generous sprinkle of paprika, thinly sliced roast beef and home-made horseradish sauce, and grated carrot and fresh hummus for the sandwich fillings. Orange and lemon zest pastry for the miniature St. Clements mince pies, ingredients for the cranberry-and-white chocolate cupcake recipe from Mrs Carter ready to be whisked up and baked in the tiny terra-cotta pots, and everything they needed to make a batch of Claudia's famous date-and-walnut scones.

"That didn't take long!" smiled Claudia, licking a splodge of whipped Irish whiskey cream from her finger. "So, what do you think about adding a French twist to the patisserie?"

"I'd love to!"

A surge of delight rushed through Millie, excited to be given the opportunity to showcase her talents to Claudia. With practised ease, she rustled up a selection of apple and calvados profiteroles, fruit tarts with champagne jelly sprinkled with popping candy, and, as a tribute to St Lucia, a dozen *Marquise au Chocolat* – mini circular chocolate mousses covered in chocolate ganache and topped with hazelnuts and a dark chocolate leaf.

"Wow! What a colourful array of desserts. I can't wait to taste them all!"

"There's one more recipe I'd like to include. Do we have time?"

"Of course! What do you have planned?"

"Could I do a Provençale twist on the *Gallette des Rois*?"

"Ah, the Cake of the Three Kings."

"Actually, at home in the south of France we always celebrate the feast of Epiphany with a *Gateau* or *Brioche des Rois*. Mum uses an old family recipe with candied orange peel, crushed pistachios and cinnamon. Jen and I loved them because instead of the standard broad bean hidden as a charm inside, Mum would hide a tiny porcelain fairy that belonged to her great-grandmother. Whoever finds it in their slice gets to wear the silver crown *and* carry the fairy's silver wand!"

"That sounds like a lovely family tradition, Millie." Then Claudia chuckled. "Did you read about the Parisian baker whose twist on the *Gallette des Rois* was a little more risqué last year?"

"I did," giggled Millie. "Not sure I'd rush to buy patisserie in the shape of a penis, though!"

When Millie finally paused to take stock of their labours she sighed with contentment at the cornucopia of culinary excellence. Suddenly, it was two o'clock and Gina and Marianne were tumbling into the kitchen, their hands full of Christmas goodies, chattering away about their morning of retail therapy in the designer boutiques of Cheltenham.

"We had the most amazing time!" declared Gina, her cheeks rosy with pleasure as she tied her apron strings around her slender waist and attached a set of cute reindeer antlers to her head. "I've even managed to get Leo a gift that I know he's going to love. But best of all, I found a bottle of vintage port for his mother. Maybe a few generous glasses might smooth away the rough edges of her sarcasm, and I'm sure she'll benefit from it too!"

Leo and Mike joined them and the second day's tutorial got underway. Millie was gratified at the way she and Claudia complemented each other, knowing instinctively when to give way to the other, or to step in to add a piece of advice or assist with a fiddlesome task.

Time flew by and before she knew it they were gathered around the table next to the French doors, clutching glasses of Champagne, staring at the assortment of sandwiches, freshly baked scones and the most dazzling array of patisserie. Everything looked wonderful showcased on the triple-tiered cake stands decorated with holly leaves and red berries, together with Claudia's best china teacups, saucers and plates with cathedral candles in silver lanterns, as they lined up for a group photograph.

Laughter and merriment rolled around the kitchen as they dug in, welcoming Tim when he arrived in the kitchen in search of a coffee after scrubbing up and looking every inch the handsome City architect in a lavender cashmere sweater, the cuffs of his white Jermyn Street shirt poking out to reveal a pair of silver compass cufflinks. He exchanged a brief complicit smile with Millie. She hadn't mentioned his accident the previous day to Claudia and he was clearly sending her a silent thank you for her discretion.

"This is the best cookery course I've been on!" declared Marianne, tucking her curls behind her ears as she selected one of Millie's exotic fruit tartlets. "And I am somewhat of an expert in that arena, aren't I, Mike?"

"You are, darling," he smirked, rolling his eyes at Leo. "What number are you up to now?"

"Let me see. I've been on an Italian desserts course with Mario Bartelli in April, An Indian Odyssey with Rav Patel in May, then there was that vegetarian one in July at Hillard Castle which was amazing. Oh, and the Spanish tapas one in August. Claudia, we did try to book on your chocolate lover's course in St Lucia and were so upset that it was fully booked that I had to make sure Mike reserved the Festive Feast course here in the Cotswolds immediately so we didn't miss out. Will you be running another cocoa-themed course in the Caribbean next year?"

"Absolutely! In fact, we're already taking bookings for the end of January. Tim and I will be going out there after the new year celebrations to start getting the villa organised for guests who want to stay as well as attend the courses."

"And we'll be adding tours of the cocoa planation, too, if you're interested," continued Tim, smiling at his wife with such affection that Millie experienced a nip of envy. She wished she could meet someone who loved her as much as Tim loved Claudia.

"A tour?" asked Marianne, pausing in her attempt to devour a profiterole whole.

"Yes. The villa used to be an old plantation house and is surrounded by cocoa palms that Tim and I and our estate manager over there have been nurturing back to health after years of neglect. The beans grown on the plantation are of exceptionally high quality. One day I hope to harvest them in sufficient quantities to make my own chocolate which I'll use in the recipes I showcase at the Paradise Cookery School."

"The Paradise Cookery School? Ah, what a wonderful name!" sighed Gina. "Count Leo and I in too, Claudia – so that's four bookings already!"

Claudia sent a smile across the table to Tim who nodded back as he sipped on his coffee. Perhaps their new venture would be just as successful as the Cotswolds Cookery School had been with the added bonus of the sunshine and a spectacular view of the Caribbean Sea.

"Of course," laughed Claudia and Millie was happy to see her friend's features relax. "Okay now. If everyone's had their fill, why don't you leave the clearing up to Millie and I and retire with your drinks to the library."

"Leo has promised to take us for a few drinks at The Flying Fox pub in the village, haven't you dear?"

"I have," smiled Leo, the creases in his forehead much less defined now that his morning of stress-filled legal negotiations was behind him. "Why don't you join us?"

"Thanks for the offer," said Tim, coming to Claudia's rescue, knowing that all she wanted to do was put her feet up after a busy day in the kitchen. "If you don't mind we'll take a rain-check. Maybe Millie could join you, though?"

"Oh, erm, no, actually I've already got a..." She had almost said *date* but changed her explanation to "...dinner invitation tonight."

"No problem," said Leo, pushing himself up from the table. "See you tomorrow for the main event, then. I'm really looking forward to discovering the secrets of producing the perfect Christmas lunch. What time do we need to be on parade, Claudia?"

"Shall we say ten a.m. sharp? Tim will be up with the larks to put the turkey in the oven, but you will be doing everything else. We'll eat at two o'clock."

"Fabulous."

Millie accepted the warm hugs of thanks from the four students and made a start on the clearing up until Claudia grabbed her arm laughing.

"Okay, Mysterious Millie. Tell me who the lucky guy is?"

"What do you... Oh, no, it's just... I'm just popping over to the lodge for a Spag Bol, that's all." She tried to appear nonchalant, but she knew that her glowing cheeks were a dead giveaway.

"I'm delighted you and Zach are cultivating the spark of friendship that ignited in St Lucia," said Claudia, beaming as she collected her into a spontaneous hug that lasted a little longer than Millie had expected. When she pulled back she could see tears glistening in Claudia's eyes. "I was a little concerned about him after Chloe left and he jumped at the chance to the swap with Jake when Jake wanted to come back to the UK while his mother was in hospital. I thought Zach was running away, but it turned out to be the best six months of his career."

"Claudia, Zach's told me about the manor. I'm so, so sorry. I know how much the place means to you both. If there's anything I can do to help, however small, then please ask."

"Oh, Millie, you are an angel, but unless you have a few spare million in your back pocket then I'm afraid it's already a done deal. Did you also hear that Dexter's arriving on Thursday afternoon with Sven Andersen for a viewing?"

"I did."

"I don't mind admitting that it'll be one of the most difficult encounters of my life. Well, apart from one." Claudia's eyes clouded for the briefest of moments. "Would you believe what my idiot of a cousin has asked us to do?"

"What?"

"Apparently, Sven is one of those crazy minimalist fanatics who like smooth white walls, clean lines and a clutter-free environment, and loathes any kind of extraneous furnishings that don't have a designer's signature scrawled on the bottom. My lovely childhood sidekick has told me to make sure the house is stripped of all its personality, so our buyer can envisage how his home in the English countryside can reflected his Scandinavian tastes. I've decluttered the lounge and dining room, there's nothing more I can do in the library, and the kitchen is almost sorted. Thankfully the switch to brunch on Thursday had worked in our favour, so once that's over I can clear everything away into the pantry ready for his visit at three."

Now Millie understood why there had been very little attempt at decorating the kitchen with a kaleidoscope of Christmas adornments for the Festive Feast course that year. It would all have had to be removed for Sven's visit.

"Claudia. How do you feel about losing the manor?"

"Of course, I'm devastated," she said, her voice tight as she set about wiping down the worktops with a vengeance. "But Tim is right, as always. It costs an absolute fortune to maintain the building, and we'll be able to use our share of the proceeds to invest in the Paradise Cookery School and that fills me with a lovely buzz of excitement. And I can't wait to see Ella again. All those emails and photographs you sent me from the Chocolate & Confetti course when I was laid up in hospital really fired my creative juices again. And there's been lots of interest in the courses, not only from the UK, but also from food lovers in America. My publisher has shown an interest in a Caribbean-themed cookery book, too – so really, it's all good."

Claudia gave Millie a bright confident smile, but there remained a shadow of sadness in the depths of her eyes. "Anyway, off you go. Get ready for your date and send my love to Zach. I hear you met his mother yesterday.

"Zach's mother? No."

"Oh, I thought Tim said you'd been to Kate's Kitchen in the village."

"Yes, we had a hot chocolate and a piece of very heavy parkin." Millie looked at Claudia as the cogs began to turn causing the muscles in her stomach to clench with panic. "Oh my God, no!"

"You didn't know that Kate was Zach's mother?"

"No! No, I did not. Oh God!"

Claudia giggled. "What's the matter?"

"I think she might have overheard me saying her cakes were lard-laden and artery-clogging."

Millie felt the heat glow in her cheeks and spread down to her chest as mortification zoomed though the catacombs of her brain. She met Claudia's gaze until her new friend and mentor burst into laughter and the two of them descended into a whirl of hilarity until tears, this time of mirth, streamed down their faces.

"Oh God, Zach must hate me!"

"I don't think that's the way I would describe Zach's feelings for you, Millie," said Claudia her expression suddenly becoming more serious. "In fact, I'd hazard a guess that you couldn't be farther from the truth."

Chapter Eleven

Millie made her way down the driveway towards Zach's home clutching a bottle of Tim's best Claret that Claudia had pressed on her with a knowing smile. Her Wellington boots were two sizes too big for her and looked ridiculous paired with her scarlet Karen Millen dress and the long gold necklace that Claudia had urged her to wear. She had always been a sun worshipper – her wardrobe was stuffed to bursting with spaghetti-strapped tops, denim shorts and Capri trousers, sparkly flip-flops and brightly coloured sarongs. She had never owned a pair of boots in her life, but perhaps now was the time to rectify that. Something else she had to work on changing.

Nerves tingled at her fingertips and not only because she intended to confront Zach about keeping the fact that Kate was his mother a secret. Her chat with Claudia in the kitchen earlier had made her realise beyond doubt that her feelings for Zach had moved on well past the friendship stage. Also, from her past experiences of spending time with Zach in the Caribbean, she wouldn't be surprised if she found him waiting on the doorstep ready to whisk her away for a night out at the greyhound track, or a climbing wall, or a choir recital at the cathedral.

But wasn't that exactly what she loved about him? That he continually challenged her to live life outside her comfort zone? That she should grab every opportunity to experience new and exciting things?

A maelstrom of emotions churned in her chest; excitement, nerves, anticipation, but also in the mix were sadness and regret that now she had met someone she would love to spend more time with, he was more than likely to be about to leave the country – par for the course as far as her love life was concerned.

A covering of snow lingered, but there had been no fresh falls and she could still see the mound of white where she had built her replica of Binks. She looked around to see if she could spot Zach's artistic contribution to Snow Sculpture of the Year but couldn't see over the wall into his back garden. She knocked on the door of the lodge and her spirits soared when she heard a bark of welcome.

"Hi Millie, come on in. Loving those boots – they really suit you."

"Thanks," she smiled, striking a supermodel's pose to showcase her footwear covered in pink daisies. She bent down to pull them off and almost laughed out loud when Zach whisked them away and hid them in the closet under the stairs.

"Come on, come through to the kitchen. "

As Zach led her down the corridor, she inhaled the delicious aroma of garlic and Italian herbs mingled with what she suspected was probably a generous soupcon of bleach. She wasn't the least bit surprised when she entered the brightly lit kitchen to see it was immaculately tidy. Every bench had been cleared of culinary paraphernalia and a glossy white table had been set with matching crockery and beautifully ironed linen. She glanced around the open-plan room into the lounge area and for a moment wondered what was bothering her until she realised that there wasn't a single Christmas decoration in sight.

Millie was about to comment on the absence of a tree, but of course she knew what Zach's answer would be – clutter! So, instead, she handed over her bottle of wine, pleased to see his eyes light up with appreciation.

"Grab a seat while I open this. Dinner's almost ready."

"Actually," said Millie, keen to deal with the elephant in the room so that its presence wouldn't interfere with her digestion. "I want to ask you why you didn't mention the fact that Kate was your mother when we were at the café yesterday. You should have let me apologise to her for the comments I made about her cuisine."

Zach laughed. "I'm sorry, Millie. I could have said something, but I can assure you that she didn't hear what you said, so what was the point of alerting her to the fact? And we were having such an enjoyable afternoon I didn't want to spoil the mood if I didn't have to and I knew you would be mortified unnecessarily. But you're absolutely right to be indignant. I'll make it up to you by introducing you formally if you like?"

"Oh, well, yes, okay," spluttered Millie, not entirely sure she was ready to be 'formally' presented to Kate, although she did wonder how he would label her when he did – random stranger, acquaintance, friend, inadvertent comedy performer… girlfriend?

She sipped her wine whilst she watched Zach empty the spaghetti into a colander and divide the pasta into two bowls before adding a generous helping of Bolognese sauce and a sprinkle of freshly grated parmesan, all finished off with a flourish of fresh basil leaves from a pot on the kitchen windowsill.

"Thank you, Zach, this looks amazing."

"Dig in."

Millie was about to do just that until she saw that Zach hadn't joined her at the table but returned to the sink to rinse the pans and the colander, dry them and return them to their rightful place in the cupboards before spraying the units with antibacterial cleanser. He smiled when he slid into the chair opposite her and raised his glass in a toast.

"To Stonelea!"

She copied his action and then inhaled her meal, complete with top-note of chlorine which reminded her of Kate's Kitchen. She now understood where Zach had acquired his fastidiousness for hygiene. However, unlike her initial thoughts on Kate's culinary prowess, Zach's cooking talents were exemplary, and she finished every last morsel.

She recalled the last time Zach had made her a spaghetti Bolognese when they'd been at Claudia's villa overlooking the bay at Soufrière on the south coast of St Lucia. It had been three weeks filled with sunshine and palm trees and friendship and new discoveries. Despite the many challenges she faced setting up the Paradise Cookery School, she had savoured every moment of the sun-filled bliss they had enjoyed together, and she wished she could teleport back there at the press of a button. The constant warmth, not only of the temperature and the infinity pool, but of the people she had met there, had made her trip to the Caribbean one of the best experiences of her life. However, she knew the overriding reason she had labelled her time there with that accolade was down to the man watching her from behind those deliciously seductive eyes, framed in the most luscious eyelashes she had seen on a man.

How she craved the chance to rekindle her friendships with Ella and her son Henri, and with Lottie and Dylan who worked at the local bar, the Purple Parrot. She even missed her daily contact with Fitz, Alph and Vic, the builders Claudia had engaged to renovate the villa's kitchen ready for their very first Paradise Cookery School guests. She had delighted in their unquestioning support of her abilities, and their encouragement that she could do anything she put her mind to, but it had been Zach's friendship that had papered over the cracks in her heart and painted the fresh canvas with a rainbow of vibrant colours to make her life sparkle again.

"Thanks for cooking dinner, Zach. Obviously, I love being in the kitchen, but sometimes it's really nice to be treated to a meal someone else has made, and that was delicious – as you can see from my plate!"

"Didn't Luke cook for you? I thought he was a chef, too?"

Millie shot a glance at Zach, taken by surprise at his mention of Luke, but gratified that she experienced no accompanying awkwardness or reluctance to share her history.

"Actually, he didn't. Funnily enough he used to live on toast and bacon sandwiches. Don't get me wrong, he enjoyed being a chef, put his heart and soul into it, but he never had that all-encompassing passion that simmers away every hour of ever day like I do, like Claudia does, and Ella does. The alchemy of food is more than a passion for some people, it's an obsession, an addiction that requires daily attention. I don't know what I would do if I couldn't have access to a kitchen. It doesn't have to be a glittering show-piece like Claudia's either. I adore the tiny kitchenette in my flat in London."

She hesitated, wondering if she should mention Zach's ex, but he'd mentioned Luke, hadn't he?

"What about Chloe? Did she like to cook?"

Zach laughed, causing Binks' ears to flicker during his snooze.

"No way. You've met Chloe. She hates doing anything that might spoil her manicure. She did make a fabulous Caesar salad though, but there's only so much lettuce a man can eat, so I used to cook during the week and we would eat out at the weekends. I bumped into her sister Louise last week in Berryford. Apparently, Chloe's working in Dubai and is loving the single lifestyle over there."

"Luke and Donna's baby is due in the new year, so his lifestyle is about to change beyond all recognition."

She took refuge in her thoughts for a moment, wondering what it would be like to be expecting the arrival of a new member of the family, not only for Luke and Donna, but for Frankie who would be getting a new half-sister or brother. She hadn't reached that stage in her life yet. However, she didn't foresee her future without children, she just wanted to wait until she was with the right person. Then something else occurred to her and she spoke her thoughts out loud before engaging her brain.

"Do Claudia and Tim not want a family? Stonelea Manor would be a fantastic place to raise children."

She saw a flash of uncertainty whip across Zach's face and wished she could have stuffed the question back in her mouth. Clearly this was another of those secrets that seemed to swirl around the manor, although she had to accept that this time it really was none of her business. However, Zach clearly knew the answer to her question and she watched him wrestle with whether to disclose a confidence.

"They'd love kids; but it just hasn't happened for them."

"Oh."

A spasm of sorrow lanced Millie's heart as she struggled to formulate a suitable response but came up with nothing that wouldn't sound trite or patronising. Fortunately, Zach had shelved his box full of witty quips and took pity on her.

"Shall we take our drinks over to the sofa?"

Zach carried the wine bottle and their glasses to the coffee table and sunk down onto the rug, his toes pointing towards the fire whilst Binks snoozed happily in front of the hearth. Millie scooted between them, grateful for the change of seating arrangements and enjoying the feeling of complete calm and relaxation that descended as they sipped the wine and stared at the dancing flames.

"So, did you always want to be a chef?"

"Not always. My first choice was a princess, but there's limited opportunities for that career path, so I plumped for the next thing on my wish list. How about you?"

"I always loved the outdoors. Before we moved to London for Dad's job, my brother and I would spend every night after school and every day in the holidays in the local fields building dens, climbing trees, damming streams and seeking out the wildlife to photograph. Dad loved his new position as a partner in a large law firm, but Mum, Callum and I hated living in the capital. Of course, Mum was devastated when she found out about his affair with Gill, but coming back here to Berryford helped us all escape the worst of the fall-out. I love it here. I love the fact that it's a community where people acknowledge each other when they pass in the street and rally round in times of need. I suppose the downside of that support is that when something upsetting happens to one of the residents, everyone feels it, even takes it personally."

"Is there no chance of the cookery school being saved?"

"I think things have gone beyond that now – unless Claudia and Tim win the lottery."

"But surely the new owner will need someone to manage the grounds. I hardly think a busy Scandi-navian celebrity millionaire would have time on his hands to mow the lawns and weed the flowerbeds."

"God, Millie, I'm not a gardener!"

"Sorry, I…"

"No, no, I'm sorry. I guess I'm more upset about what's happened than I think. Sven Andersen has his own staff that have been vigorously vetted and can be trusted. It's part of the deal that he doesn't want to be lumbered with any of Stonelea's current employees. And it's not just me who'll be losing their job, there're two full-time gardeners, and Claudia employs a local cleaning company too, but I'm the only one who'll be losing their home."

"Will you stay with your mum?"

"No."

"Zach, I'm so...."

A sudden spasm of desire rippled down her spine as she felt Zach's warm breath on her neck. Without her realising, he had moved closer, his lips millimetres from her earlobe and her imagination flew down the tunnel of pleasure, conjuring up a delicious contemplation of shared secrets. He studied her with such scorching intensity that her heart pounded out a symphony of exhilaration and the hairs on her forearms prickled with expectation.

She lowered her gaze to his lips, so close to hers, then back up to his eyes which mirrored the feelings she was experiencing, but also held a question. If she risked breathing, the moment would be broken so she inched forward, her anticipation building that at last they were about to revisit the wonderful kisses they had shared under the swaying palm trees in the Caribbean sunshine. To her surprise and utter disappointment, she saw a flicker of hesitation, a hint of uncertainty, stalk across Zach's face, and he severed their connection, leaning forward to give Binks a brief pat before making his way to the kitchen and setting the kettle to boil.

The pendulum of emotions in Millie's chest swung from the height of delight to the depths of despondency. What had just happened? If she had leaned forward another couple of inches she would be kissing Zach now and she knew there was nothing she would rather do. Could she have misread the signals? She didn't think so. There was no mistaking the fizz of mutual attraction that had reverberated in the space between them. She was confused.

In an attempt to disguise her bewilderment, she pushed herself up from the rug and resettled herself on the wrinkled leather Chesterfield to watch Zach prepare their coffees with military precision. When he handed Millie her drink, he averted his eyes.

However, Millie was no longer the insecure victim she had been when Luke had ditched her. If Zach had taught her anything it was that honesty and openness were the most desirable qualities in the arena of relationships and she couldn't contemplate leaving the lodge without understanding what had just happened between them and why.

"Zach…"

"Millie…"

"No, you go."

"Okay." Zach exhaled a long sigh, sliding onto the seat beside her and welcoming Binks onto his lap. "I haven't told Claudia and Tim yet, but I received a job offer last week."

"You have? Where?"

"Scotland."

"Scotland?"

Millie's heart dropped like a stone down a well before bouncing back into her chest where it lodged like a concrete slab. Suddenly Blake's comments about Scotland the day before made perfect sense. So that was it, that was why he'd said they had 'things to talk about' in that last text he'd sent her before she'd left London for Berryford, why he'd pulled away from her when she'd thought they were about to kiss. He was uncertain about his future and wanted to avoid starting something they couldn't finish, because Scotland might as well be the Caribbean for the time it would take to commute for a weekend in London, or vice versa.

"Oh, well… that's great news, isn't it?"

"If you like the wind-swept Western Isles, then yes, it's good news."

In that moment she was able to read her feelings perfectly. The emotions that had been born in Soufrière and flourished into friendship, had blossomed over the interceding months into something deeper that had crystallised when they had reconnected in Berryford. She wanted to spend every spare second getting to know Zach better, to spend time learning what he did in his working life and inviting him to stay in her attic room above Étienne's. Now it seemed it was too late. Their chance of a possible future together had been extinguished by the arrival of a wealthy entrepreneur who hated clutter with a vengeance and wanted to convert the manor house into a high security home in which to shelter from the limelight.

"Are you sure there's no way Claudia and Tim can keep the house? What if…"

Zach's eyes softened. "Millie, don't you think Claudia and Tim have explored every avenue possible? Tim told me that he's tried to persuade Dexter to hold off for another six months, they even offered to sell the villa, but Dexter needs the cash straight away. He's told them it's because he's made some bad investments, but I think it's more than that."

"What do you mean?"

"Oh, nothing sinister. It's just that Dexter lives on the other side of the world. He only has memories of a childhood here, so no real knowledge or connection with the people who live here now. He has no interest in how the change of ownership will affect everyone in the village because he hasn't been back since Claudia's father's funeral ten years ago when

Claudia inherited her share of the estate and he agreed to her cookery school idea."

"Maybe when Claudia has the chance to talk to him face-to-face on Thursday, she'll be able to explain all that to him and he could change his mind."

"I don't think so. Sven's money will be within his grasp - unless someone else comes up with a couple of million and that's not going to happen."

Despite the fact that she had only just arrived in Berryford, Millie craved the chance to do something to help, to keep the Stonelea Manor as a cookery school, to maintain the traditions of the village, but most of all she was desperate for Zach to stay in the Cotswolds, to keep his job and his home where he and Binks were so clearly happy.

The mood in the room had morphed from merry to melancholic and a surge of annoyance wove through Millie's veins. Why did Dexter have to be so selfish? But following immediately was the realisation that it was none of her business what Dexter did, or wanted, or needed, which made her sad.

"Come on. Binks and I will walk you back down to the manor. You've got an early start tomorrow. I'm sure the cookery part will go without a hitch, not so sure about the state of the kitchen though!"

Zach tried to add his usual twist of mischief to his comment but his heart clearly wasn't in it. Everyone was allowed a moment of relief from constant positivity and Millie knew that the imminent change in his future path, both professional and personal, was obviously weighing heavily on his mind.

Binks sensed the change in atmosphere and leapt up from his resting place, trotting to the coat stand to fetch his lead for his final walk of the day. Millie was about to offer to help with the washing up, but of course, the kitchen was already spotless, which for some unfathomable reason caused tears to prick at the back of her eyes. Just as she felt she had turned the corner on her reluctance to embark on a new relationship, the optimism rug had been whipped from beneath her feet.

She would miss Zach more than she had ever expected.

Chapter Twelve

The Christmas Lunch Festive Feast tutorial was a triumph. Even Mike managed to make a very competent attempt at 'from-scratch' Yorkshire puddings – although they did look like flat cupcakes. Everything went smoothly because Claudia and Tim had spent the night before preparing everything; setting the table in the dining room with the best china and polishing the crystal glasses and silver cutlery which shone beneath the very modern chandelier that had been a wedding gift from Tim's parents. Garlands of shiny green holly snaked around the mantlepiece, the aroma of spicy cloves lingered in the air, and the whole room looked very festive.

Millie struggled all day to shove her negative thoughts about Zach leaving into the far crevices of her mind so that their guests could enjoy the highlight of the week at Stonelea Manor without wondering what was bothering Claudia's co-presenter. She hoped she had pulled it off because Claudia had been on top form, recounting anecdotes of TV and radio interviews she had given over the years, mishaps that had happened on research trips she had taken to exotic locations, as well as bouncing around ideas for future courses at the Paradise Cookery School. If Millie hadn't known about the imminent arrival of Dexter and Sven, she would never have guessed that Claudia was about to lose the home her family had owned and loved for over seventy years. Even Tim had been jovial company, regaling his avid audience with stories about his inventions and promising to show Leo and Mike how far he'd got with his lawn mower whilst studiously avoiding looking in Claudia's direction.

Millie set down a jug of home-made brandy sauce to accompany the fragrant Christmas pudding that adorned the middle of the table like a piece of culinary art. In a nod to the desserts she had created in St Lucia, she had also made a huge passionfruit and mango pavlova with a froth of whipped cream in case Gina or Marianne preferred something less heavy after the main course.

"Okay, dig in everyone!"

"Oh, I can't decide which to have," announced Mike, twisting his lips in indecision.

"Why not have a slice of each?" coaxed Claudia.

"Great idea," declared Tim, reaching out for the serving spoon, his eyes wide with relish.

In the end they all had seconds and Millie thought if she consumed another mouthful she would burst, until she saw the cheeseboard that had been Tim's responsibility and noticed a particularly good Roquefort, in her view the king of French cheeses.

"Well, that was the best Festive Feast I have ever had!" declared Leo, pushing back his chair and rubbing his stomach in satisfaction as Claudia brought two cafetières of Blue Mountain coffee to the table along with a box of After Eight mints. "Gina, I just know we're going to nail Christmas dinner this year. What do you think?"

"Definitely," she laughed, her hazel eyes sparkling as she leaned forward to kiss her husband, her cheeks sporting red dots of delight. "I don't know about you, but I need a lie down after all that food."

"Me too," giggled Marianne, wiggling her eyebrows and sending a suggestive glance in Mike's direction as they helped to clear the table of the dessert plates and cheeseboard.

Millie deposited the crockery in the sink and ran her eyes despondently over the washing up as their guests trotted off up the stairs, chattering away about their plans for the rapidly approaching festive break.

"Well, that went amazingly well. Thanks Millie, I couldn't have done it without your help."

"I thoroughly enjoyed it, and I learned a great deal too. Would you believe it's the first time I've made a traditional English Christmas dinner?"

Millie glanced at Claudia who had taken on the appearance of a deflated balloon, her earlier buoyancy vanished into a chasm of tiredness. Her heart performed a flip-flop of sympathy and she smiled at her new friend and mentor.

"Look, why don't you go upstairs and take a nap too? I'll finish up here."

"I can't leave you with all this to sort out!"

"It's no problem. You might have noticed that I'm not the tidiest of cooks, but I'm on a journey of self-improvement guided by my friend and colleague at Étienne's, Poppy, and ably encouraged by my sister, Jen. I'm used to blitzing a room after a cookery session." She laughed, then softened her expression as she scrutinised Claudia's face, not surprised to witness a surge of relief flick across her expression.

"If you're sure?"

"Absolutely. I'll see you tomorrow for the brunch tutorial and if you need any help with decluttering the house before Dexter and Sven arrive, then I'm at your disposal, although I see that you've already done most of the hard work."

"There's just the kitchen to sort out after tomorrow's tutorial, and Tim thinks we should take down the tree in the hallway, too. It's ridiculous that we've got to go to so much trouble to impress a buyer. Surely he should have enough vision to see beyond the décor!"

"Don't ask me, I prefer a house filled with as much bric-a-brac and souvenirs of a life well lived as possible! The more the merrier, in fact. It's just so much more homely, especially at Christmas."

Claudia looked as though she was about to say something else but instead she squeezed Millie's hand, gave her a weak smile, and disappeared upstairs with an exhausted Tim in tow. After all, he had been up at the crack of dawn to put the turkey in the oven.

Millie sighed as she contemplated the task ahead of her, but she had seen worse, much worse. She pulled on a pair of Marigolds, tuned in the radio to a channel playing non-stop Christmas songs, and started to hand-wash the crystal before loading up the dishwasher with the pots and pans and utensils. With the music providing a rhythm to work to, the kitchen was spotless in no time and Millie was so proud of herself that she took a quick snap to send to Poppy as evidence of her achievement.

She was about to press send on her text when she paused, a swift kick of homesickness hitting her in the abdomen. She was suddenly desperate to hear Poppy's voice, to hear all about her date with the hunky French sculptor and her plans for the Mistletoe Ball.

"Hi Poppy, it's Millie."

"Hey, Millie, great to hear from you! How's things going at the showbiz end of the profession?"

Millie laughed, overwhelmed with delight to be speaking to her friend. "Everything's going well. The guests on the course are great and I'm loving working with Claudia. I'm working hard on the lessons you've taught me on the subject of tidiness, and to prove it I've sent you a couple of photographs. You'd love Claudia's kitchen, Pop, it's amazing!"

"I'm so jealous! We're run off our feet here with the Christmas trade. Étienne has even deigned to appear front-of-house to help out, but it's not helping with his temper. Why are you French people so temperamental?"

"Passionate, we call it," giggled Millie, aware that her French accent had grown stronger as she became more animated in her excitement at being able to talk to Poppy. Of course, it was also more evident over the telephone too.

"Talking of passionate, spill the details Harper!"

"What details?"

"Don't give me that. I've seen the photos of the broodingly handsome Zach Barker, remember! Are the two of you curled up in a little love nest, hiding from the snow in front of a roaring log fire, feeding each other morsels of mince pies and knocking back the Champers?"

"Actually…"

"Oh my God! You are!"

"We are not!"

"But something's going on I can tell from your voice. Come on, Millie, humour me. François still hasn't accepted my invitation to the ball at the weekend; he clearly likes to keep a girl dangling until she's finished her chiselled masterpiece – although masterpiece might not be the best description for my disastrous attempt at recreating my favourite child-hood pet, Barnaby, in stone."

Millie suddenly wanted to divulge every detail of her dinner date with Zach and seek her friend's sage advice. After all, she did have a mountain of experience in the romance arena. She launched in, embroidering the tale with humour to conceal her uncertainty about how Zach felt about her.

"So he didn't kiss you?"

"No. I think he was going to, but something stopped him at the last minute. You know, after what happened with Luke, I really don't want to get involved with someone who keeps secrets. I need honesty, even when the truth might hurt, it's better than skulking around, avoiding talking about what's important."

"But hadn't Zach just told you that he'd landed a new job in Scotland?"

"Yes."

"Do you think he could have been reluctant to progress things in order to protect you? With the best will in the world, it's difficult to continue a relationship when one party lives in another country."

Millie sighed, gratitude for Poppy's friendship washing over her like a warm comfort blanket.

"You're right, Poppy. Thanks for being my love guru!"

Of course, Zach wouldn't want to embark on a new relationship when he was about to make a fresh start, whether that was in Scotland or the Caribbean, and if she had taken the time to think things through, she would have understood that. All Zach had been doing was protecting her – and himself.

The realisation that his behaviour had nothing to do with his feelings for her didn't fill her with relief but with sadness that any hope of having Zach in her life on a permanent basis had been crushed. Her emotions tumbled painfully, like one of Tim's broken washing machines, so she quickly changed the subject, asking for all the gossip on the other members of Étienne's team which Poppy recounted with gusto.

As she climbed the stairs to her suite, she resolved to discard her regret that her future probably wouldn't include Zach, and to enjoy every moment she could spend in his company. She reminded herself that his cheerful, quirky and mischievous personality had been the bright star in her all-encompassing gloom when she'd arrived heartbroken in St Lucia, and that she had never expected to find such solace in the sun, let alone meet someone who would teach her how to be happy again. How, by approaching life with a braced sword of optimism, gave the bearer more than an equal chance of winning the battle.

Chapter Thirteen

Dawn was only just beginning to breach the horizon when Millie woke. Again, she had slept well and tossed back the covers to leap into the day with a spring in her step until reality crashed into her thoughts. Dexter would be arriving at three o'clock and there was a great deal to do before the house was ready to show its face to its potential new owner. She wanted to save Claudia from as much work as possible, so she left her curls to dry naturally, using a trick Ella had taught her in the Caribbean to tackle the frizz by running a splodge of coconut oil all the way from root to tip. She pulled on a pair of smart black trousers and a crimson sweater with snowflakes on the front and cantered down the staircase.

Every time she walked into Stonelea's kitchen a burst of pleasure erupted in her heart. It was a truly amazing place and she was gutted for Claudia that she was about to lose it. She started to prepare the ingredients for that day's tutorial into six separate sets of bowls to make the presentation as easy as possible to follow. The DJ of the local radio station was playing a non-stop medley of jaunty Christmas tunes causing her hips to sway, and as she inhaled the delicious aromas of cinnamon and buttery pastry her sprits ballooned. She really was at her happiest when indulging in a frenzy of baking-related activities.

Nine o'clock came and went and there was no sign of Claudia. The tutorial was due to start at nine thirty so that the food they prepared would be ready for brunch at eleven. Millie set out the ingredients on the respective workstations and stood back to survey her hard work.

"Wow, this all looks fabulous!" declared Marianne, her green eyes shining as she paused briefly at the kitchen door before striding straight to the drawer that contained the freshly laundered aprons. "You know, I've told Mike that instead of keeping our place in Marbella as a holiday home - which we get to visit once or twice a year if we're lucky - we should invest in a something like this, but on a smaller scale, obviously. When I spoke to Claudia about it yesterday, she told me to go for it. Did you know that before she set up the Paradise Cookery School in St Lucia, she'd been thinking of expanding her repertoire here by organising courses aimed at the younger generation – a Cool Kids Cookery Course in the Cotswolds?"

"No, I didn't…"

"Well, I think it's a great idea. It's really important to teach our children to cook healthy meals – and it's a much more valuable life skill than learning to speak French or Spanish, in my opinion. She should definitely run a few courses in the school holidays."

"I agree," smiled Millie, trying to disguise her reaction so that Marianne didn't ask any more questions about the future plans of the school. She didn't want to lie to her, but she knew Claudia wouldn't want her private business about the imminent demise of the whole Claudia Croft Cookery School being made public. She decided to change the subject. "Where's Mike?"

"On his way down, don't worry. He won't miss this session – he loves brunch. We never miss an opportunity to indulge on a Sunday morning, sitting at our kitchen table with the newspapers. It's the only time we get to relax together without interruptions. The working week is so full-on, then Saturdays are spent rushing around catching up on chores and entertaining – so Sunday is sacrosanct. I wish we had more time to do that, actually. Ah, here he is. Mike, I was just telling Millie that I'd love to run a cookery school at our villa. Oh, and I'd have embroidered aprons and chef's hats and give everyone a file filled with laminated recipe cards to take home afterwards. Oh, and we'd do healthy Spanish tapas and…"

"Morning everyone. I'm starving," interrupted Leo as he strode towards the coffee machine accompanied by a waft of spicy aftershave. "Can't wait to get stuck in and sample today's brunch. Then, my friends, I have a treat planned for us." Leo's eyes sparkled with excitement.

"What?" asked Gina, following him into the kitchen, grabbing a slice of home-made panettone on the way past.

"It wouldn't be a surprise if I told you, would it? But trust me, you're going to love it."

Millie smiled. Leo had confided in her at the beginning of the week that he had scored four Grand Circle tickets for the pantomime in Oxford that night. They were going to enjoy an evening of unbridled theatrical fun before going out for dinner. She knew they'd have a great time.

Millie glanced at the clock and then at the door into the hallway. It was nine forty-five and a coil of concern had begun to weave through her chest as she wondered why Claudia hadn't arrived yet.

"Okay, so today we'll be preparing Eggs Benedict with the best hollandaise sauce you've ever tasted and finished with a dash of caviar. Then, we'll rustle up a delicious smoked salmon and mascarpone tortilla before moving on to the Brioche French toast which we'll serve with thinly sliced bananas and warm salted caramel sauce. Why don't you make a start on chopping the pistachios for the Stollen muffins and I'll be back in a minute?"

Aware that Gina and Marianne were gaping in surprise at her unexpected exit, Millie dashed out of the kitchen and was halfway up the stairs when she bumped into Tim on the landing, his face paler than she had seen, his dark pewter eyes creased in concern.

"Tim? Is everything okay?"

"Actually, I was just coming to see you. I'm sorry but Claudia has spent most of the night in the bathroom. Looks like she's come down with a winter vomiting bug. She's upset but I've insisted that she rests and she's just fallen asleep. Could you handle the tutorial by yourself today? I'm available if you need any help."

"Oh, poor Claudia. Do you think you should call the doctor?"

"I suggested the very same thing, but she's adamant that it's a twenty-four-hour virus and she'll be as right as rain when she's slept it off. Of course, like all these things, it couldn't have come at a worst time, what with Dexter and Sven on their way down from London, but best laid plans and all that. I told Claudie that I'm more than capable of performing the required estate agent duties. I *have* been a bloody architect for the last twenty-five years!"

Tim ran his fingers through his thick hair causing it to appear even more bouffant that usual. He pinned a determined smile on his face and met Millie's eyes.

"Alright, lead the way, Chef! I've always wondered what it would be like to be a sous chef for the day. Claudia has consistently refused to indulge me – she's seen my workshop and thinks I'll trash her kitchen, which is an opinion I have to say I find rather insulting, even if it is based on fact."

"Tim, it's no problem if you would rather stay with Claudia. I can manage – in fact, I've already done all the preparation, it's just a matter of the presentation and the eating."

"Even better – they are the best bits. Come on!"

Tim strode into the kitchen like a silver-haired Marco Pierre White, strapped on one of Claudia's signature aprons and stood at the presentation work-bench like a professor behind a lectern eyeing his students over his spectacles.

"Hello, everyone. I'm afraid Claudia is feeling a little under the weather this morning, so I'm delighted to inform you that Millie has agreed to take on the starring role today, ably supported by Yours Truly. Take it away, Millie!"

Trying hard not to giggle at Tim's rather show-biz introduction, Millie launched into delivering the fourth Festive Feast course of the week, grateful that brunch was one of the easiest meals to guide their guests through. Once the Stollen muffins were safely baking in the oven and the aroma of ground almonds and melting marzipan filled the air, the group set about making the Brioche French toast.

"Ah, if there is one fragrance that screams Christmas it's cinnamon," sighed Gina, licking her fingertips and rolling her eyes in exaggerated ecstasy.

"And cloves," said Marianne, whose hair sported a sprinkling of the edible glitter she had used to finish off her blueberry-cream tea bread that had been baked in a Bundt tin and drizzled with a generous helping of lemon icing.

"Or a hot rum toddy," added Mike, who had made an early start on the brandy that Millie had brought from the library to add to the sweet mincemeat.

Tim proved to be an entertaining and hilarious co-presenter and laughter reverberated around the room from the off. He looked like he'd stepped into the shoes of an inept inventor, cooking up madcap experiments and causing even more culinary chaos than Millie was used to, which was certainly saying something.

Millie had intended the champagne for the Buck's Fizz to be opened when they sat down to eat, but Gina had other ideas and before long she and Marianne were giggling and teasing Tim about showcasing his wacky contraptions on Dragon's Den. They encouraged even more outrageous shenanigans involving a sieve and a large commercial bag of flour that turned his hair and most of the workbench into a snow-topped scene, intersperse with dots of custard-yellow sauce and sliced boiled egg.

Leo was the only member of the group sober enough, and sensible enough, to complete his brunch to any reasonable standard, but he played his part in the comedy show by displaying his skills as an accomplished impersonator of a selection of famous TV chefs, observing their various quirks perfectly. By the time they sat down at the table, they were all ravenous and every morsel was devoured swiftly with lip-smacking appreciation.

"So, come on Tim, why don't you show me this workshop of yours," urged Mike, pushing back his chair and making his way towards the boot room door. "Are you really working on a solar-powered ride-on lawn mower?"

"I am..."

Millie rolled her eyes as the three men disappeared into the courtyard. Standing at the kitchen window, she followed their progress across the cobbles, smiling as Tim unlocked the huge padlock and wrenched the door of his workshop open with an exaggerated flourish. Gina and Marianne excused themselves to get ready for their afternoon 'treat' and Millie was able at last to survey the kitchen through fresh eyes.

It was like another episode from the Cotswold Culinary Catastrophe. Detritus was strewn across every available surface: bags of flour, slices of French toast, empty egg cartons, coffee beans, escaped pistachios, a dusting of ground ginger. Cutlery drawers had been opened and baking trays balanced on them, saucepans and measuring jugs piled high in the sinks.

She knew Zach had christened her Messy Millie, but Tim really did take the accolade of the Most Untidy Cook she had encountered in her career to date. She opened the door of the pantry, probably her favourite room in the house – a miniature bazaar of culinary preparations that sent ripples of supreme joy through her veins whenever she entered its hallowed space. She could spend hours, no weeks, in there and still crave an extra few minutes, but now wasn't the time. She had to hide everything away before Dexter arrived with his guest.

Millie sighed and reached for her Marigolds, determined to scrub, wipe and polish until the kitchen shone, but before she could splosh a generous splash of disinfectant into her bucket she heard the front door open and an unfamiliar voice call out for Claudia. Her stomach performed a swift pirouette of panic because the enquiry held a distinct Australian twang.

God! Dexter had arrived early!

She could only pray that Sven wasn't following in his wake. Sadly, her guardian angel had clocked off duty because when she turned round there were two, well-groomed men hovering in the doorway, clearly reluctant to set foot into the chaotic kitchen for fear of getting their immaculate attire dirty. The smaller guy with trendy tortoiseshell glasses, sandy-coloured hair and a dimple in the middle of his clean-shaven chin, was the first to speak whilst his friend looked on like a gobsmacked goldfish.

"Oh my God! What happened in here? It looks like a flour bomb's exploded. Where's Claudia?"

Millie fleetingly considered running across the courtyard to alert Tim, but her manners forced her to walk towards Dexter, her hand outstretched.

"Hello, you must be Claudia's cousin, Dexter. I'm Amelia Harper – Claudia engaged me to help her present the Festive Feast cookery course this week."

"But where is she?"

Dexter's eyes widened as they landed on the pyramid of dirty plates and cups piled next to the sink and abandoned on the draining board ready for their twirl in the dishwasher.

"She's…"

Millie glanced at the second man, his expression speaking volumes as he remained on the threshold, his upper lip curled in distaste. There was a touch of arrogance about the way he held his head, his electric blue eyes sharp and alert for the possible unwelcome approach of a rogue paparazzo. Taller than Dexter by at least four inches, with the most perfectly sculpted cheekbones and bleached blond hair teased professionally into spikes, she understood immediately how he had reached the dizzying heights of Sweden's celebrity circus. Despite the revulsion evident on his face, he oozed charisma from every pore – it was just that it wasn't directed at her. He obviously had an on-off switch and today it was resolutely switched off.

"I'm sorry, Claudia's indisposed."

Ergh, thought Millie. She sounded like a Victorian governess, but that was the first word that had come into her head. She didn't know how close Claudia and Dexter were after everything that had happened recently and had no idea whether he would rush upstairs to sit at her bedside and stroke her fevered brow or avoid the room like the plague.

"So you've stepped into her shoes?"

"Yes, I…"

"What's the matter with you? Haven't you heard of tidying up as you go along?" demanded Sven, fixing her with the most malevolent gaze.

Millie cringed as she realised that Sven belonged firmly to the irritating segment of the people spectrum. She knew it was the contents of his heart that had suddenly created the semblance of weasel-like features in her mind's eye, because without his declared intentions to change Stonelea beyond recognition, she would have probably described him as handsome.

"Yes, of course I have, and I was just about to..."

"Where's Tim? He's supposed to be expecting us and he promised he would have everything ready for the tour..."

Maybe it was the way Sven was snarling at her like she was some kind of inconvenient minion who had no right to be in Claudia's kitchen, an imposter who had little idea what she was doing. Or maybe it was because she experienced a sudden surge of indignation that she *did* have the right credentials to be standing where she was. Whichever it was, she decided to interrupt Dexter's flow.

"If I remember correctly, you were expected at three o'clock and it's now..." she glanced overtly at the clock above the refrigerator, "twelve fifty-five. You are over two hours early."

Dexter opened his mouth to respond but thought better of it and turned to lead Sven back into the hallway – currently devoid of the magnificent

Christmas tree to accommodate Sven's declared loathing of all household adornments.

"We'll wait in the library..." began Dexter, clearly a little flustered at the unexpected turn of events.

Millie saw his fingers tremble when he seized the brass door handle of Claudia's favourite room, and a spasm of empathy erupted deep in her chest. She knew in that moment that Dexter had been forced into the situation of selling Stonelea Manor by the people he owed money to. She just wished he had been able to find a purchaser who would continue with the traditions of the village, and not this would-be recluse who intended to turn the place into something akin to a high security prison.

"And bring us some coffee," ordered Sven, and without registering Millie's jaw-drop, the men retreated to Claudia's sanctuary.

The sound of their footsteps on the parquet flooring left a residue of distress in Millie's heart. Well, as viewings go, that hadn't started off so well, she thought as she set the kettle to boil and rinsed out the cafetière. She briefly considered the tin of rat poison she had noticed in the cupboard under the sink but discarded the thought as impractical – eliminating Sven would only provide a temporary reprieve to Claudia and Tim's problems. A spark of sorrow ignited in her heart when she thought of the uptight, obnoxious millionaire becoming the new owner of the home in which Claudia and Tim had invested all their hopes and dreams.

She delivered the cafetière, along with a plate of sliced blueberry cream tea bread left over from brunch, to the library, feeling like the hired help. She was tempted to serve the coffee in Sven's lap, but even she had to admit that sullying those impeccable Armani trousers would have been sacrilege. She could only hope that the sticky lemon icing would be so irresistible that Sven wouldn't be able to stop himself from licking his fingers and allowing his mouth to twist into something approaching a smile— although somehow she doubted that had happened since he was a toddler.

"Where did you say Tim was?" asked Dexter, without even thanking her for the coffee.

"In his workshop."

Oh, God! Should she have said that? She knew Claudia had instructed Tim, under pain of death, to exclude his den from the Stonelea Manor Grand Tour.

"Right."

Dexter slung back his black coffee and rose to his feet, stress pulling at the corners of his lips. "Come on, Sven. I'll introduce you to my cousin's husband and we'll get this show on the road."

Sven simply nodded.

Clearly a man of few words, thought Millie, wondering whether it was because he saved his voice for more worthy causes, whether he thought her undeserving of his attention, or if he was still in a state of shock from the kitchen fiasco. Surely a bit of clutter couldn't render a person near mute! She almost crumbled into hysteria when she saw him remove a bottle of hand sanitiser and rub a generous coating over his hands. Was she mistaken or had his faced blanched at the sight of the higgledy-piggledy image of Claudia's well-stocked library shelves?

Instead of guiding Sven through the kitchen to Tim's workshop, Dexter sensibly decided to take a detour via the front door and round the west wing of the house to the courtyard, regaling his friend with a monologue of information about the more positive aspects of the exterior architecture like a super-powered robot estate agent.

Millie followed them as far as the door, her heart pounding out a cacophony of panic. Despite her trepidation over what was about to ensue, she still paused for a moment to drink in the bucolic landscape outside. The sun was struggling to remain above the treetops, but still managed to send slithers of bright light through the clouds, circling the whole scene with a golden halo. In her humble opinion, if

Sven was unable to look beyond the surface to see the beauty beyond, then he didn't deserve to own such a slice of magnificence.

Millie wasn't sure what to do. Should she retreat to the kitchen and either hide in the pantry until the whole episode was over, or make a start on the tidying up in the hope that it would be pristine and daisy-fresh when Dexter and Sven returned? Or should she take the shortcut through the boot room and warn Tim that they were on their way?

What would Claudia do?

She decided to warn Tim. She sprinted to the back door and out into the courtyard only to find that Dexter and Sven were within yards of the workshop entrance; two tall blond men, elegantly dressed in immaculately-cut designer suits and matching over-coats with velvet collars; Dexter's navy blue, Sven's a dark charcoal grey. Sven had added a pair of leather gloves, probably to protect himself from potential contact with germs. Millie was suddenly reminded of a pair of undertakers and only a flock of revolving crows was needed to complete the ominous picture.

Her ears pricked up as she listened in to their conversation.

"So, completion at the end of January?"

"Sure. The funds are available as soon as you tell me the house has been vacated. The bulldozers will be on standby from the first."

A nip of dread shot through Millie's veins. Had she heard right? Had Sven actually said the word bulldozers? Oh, God, could Dexter have made a *worse* choice for the new owner of Stonelea Manor?

She hurried to catch the men up and arrived outside the workshop at the same time they did. Dexter glanced at her in irritation as he opened the door to be presented with a view of Leo and Mike's buttocks as they bent over to inspect Tim's pride and joy, the upturned remote-controlled, solar-powered, ride-on lawn mower.

"Excuse me? Who are you?" asked Dexter, a faint hint of panic in his tone.

Leo turned around, a ready smile on his lips, his hand extended to greet the new arrivals, but his smile faded when he registered the expression of belligerence on Sven's face.

"Leo Groves, of Groves and Hindmarsh," he said, a formal note creeping into his voice. "This is my business partner, Mike Sanderson."

Mike stepped forward, his bulk forcing Dexter and Sven to retreat a few steps into the courtyard, causing Millie to take an unexpected stride backwards where her heel connected with a loose cobble and she tumbled to the ground, landing on her bottom with a loud *harmph*.

In an instant, she was righted by a strong pair of hands. From the whiff of lemony cologne, she knew immediately that Zach had come to her aid and the tension that had been rising in her body melted. She watched him swiftly take everything in and swing into action.

"Perhaps you'd be better having this meeting in the house?"

"Ah, Zach," said Dexter, offering him his palm. "I..."

But he got no further. An almighty explosion wrenched the air, sending debris flying into the courtyard and everyone running for cover. Zach wasted no time rushing into the workshop, fighting his way through upended spades, buckets, pitchforks, brooms and ancient, rust-covered garden implements like an explorer in virgin jungle, until he reached the side of a very dazed Tim.

Millie was inches behind him, taking in the wide-eyed surprise on Tim's face as he surveyed his beloved workshop in distress. Relief seeped through her body when she saw he was unhurt but doused in a generous coating of vivid green powder that made him look like the Incredible Hulk's more puny brother. With Leo and Mike's help, Zach escorted Tim through the jumble of tools into the courtyard – just in time to witness the whole of the workshop's roof tumble down in their wake, sending a cloud of silver dust into the sky that then rained down on the audience like grey snow.

Ergh!" exclaimed Sven, covering his hair with his forearms, turning his back on the fallout, and making a dash for the boot room, with Dexter, Leo and Mike close behind him.

Millie was about to follow everyone into the library when she felt her phone buzz in her pocket. She removed it and glanced at the screen, smiling at Zach.

"My sister, Jen. I'll catch you up."

She began walking up the stairs so she could take her call in private.

Chapter Fourteen

"Hello?"

"Oh, Millie, thank God! I've been ringing you for the last half hour!"

"Hi, Jen. Sorry, things have been a bit manic around here. Would you believe Tim has just almost blown himself up and the worst thing is…"

"Yes, yes," interrupted Jen, a wobble in her voice. "Is Claudia with you?"

"No. Why?"

"Are you sitting down?"

"What do you mean? *Should* I sit down?"

"It would probably be best if you did."

"Oh, no! Is it Mum? Please tell me it's not Mum?"

"It's not Mum, but you do need to prepare yourself for a shock."

"A shock. Are the girls…"

"The girls are fine."

"Jen, will you please just tell me what's going on? I can't stand the suspense."

Millie had reached the top of the stairs and sunk down on the top step, staring straight ahead at the spectacular gallery of oil paintings as she stole herself to hear her sister's news.

"I really would have preferred to have been with you when I told you, but I don't want you to see it first on social media so…"

"Jen! For heaven's sake!"

"Luke has just announced the birth of his baby. It's a girl and they've called her Alice."

"Oh."

Millie scrambled around for something suitable to say in response, but she discovered that her brain had spontaneously been washed of all cogent thought. Of course, she'd known that Luke and Donna's baby was due soon, but she had never been presented with a similar scenario upon which to base an appropriate reaction.

Over the last six months, she had tried hard not to dwell on Luke's imminent parenthood because even though she had moved on from the heartbreak he had caused, she couldn't forget that during the last few weeks of their relationship, leading up to her engagement party when the affair had been made public, Donna had been pregnant with Luke's child, and that hurt.

"Millie? Are you still there? Millie?"

"It's okay, Jen. I'm still here."

The strain evident in her voice made her sound like a strangled duck. She tried to swallow, but the acidic taste at the back of her throat caused her to gag.

"How do you feel, darling?"

Jen's tone was gentle, sympathetic, the same voice she used when one of Millie's nieces needed comforting after a fall. She fervently wished her sister was sitting next to her on the step, armed with a plaster and a loving hug to make the pain go away. But she wasn't seven years old, she was a grown-up and, like it or not, she had to deal with whatever life threw at her. She had two choices; either she could crumble into a sniffling mess or she could straighten her shoulders, draw in a deep, fortifying breath and work on her forgiveness skills.

She briefly toyed with the first option as she explored her emotions to come up with an appropriate response to her sister's enquiry. Her stomach muscles had contracted around something akin to a pineapple, and her chest felt as though a block of concrete was squeezing the air from her lungs which made her feel lightheaded.

"I'm... I'm fine."

"If you need me to come over to Berryford I can be with you in a couple of hours. Or if you wanted to come to us, I'm sure Claudia will understand when you explain what's happened. You've only got Friday's farewell cocktail party tomorrow so I'm sure she'll be able to manage without you."

"No, no, I couldn't do that…"

Suddenly the cloud of confusion lifted, and she was able to put the whole thing into perspective. Claudia and Tim were facing a much more upsetting scenario – not only losing their business but losing their home and the support of their friends, yet they were facing the prospect with dignity and positivity for what the future could hold elsewhere. That was what she had to do.

As she sat on the step, listening to her sister's soothing words, she realised that her reaction had been that of surprise rather than upset. She didn't love Luke anymore and he had every right to make a new life with someone else, including having a family. With the benefit of hindsight, she realised that they hadn't been the perfect fit she had thought they were and she was grateful to him for terminating their relationship, although she would have preferred it if he could have done that as a soon as he had met Donna and realised she was the one, and certainly not at their engagement party.

"I'm really okay, Jen."

"Sure?"

"Yes. I haven't had chance to talk to you about it, but over the last six months I've learned a lot about myself and I've realised that while I had thought Luke was my soulmate, he didn't make my heart sing or my emotions fizz as much as…"

She stopped, relishing the curl of happiness zipping around her body and causing a smile to stretch her lips.

"As much as what?"

Millie glanced down to the bottom of the stairs and her heart performed a flip–flop of pleasure when she saw Zach staring up at her.

"As much as what?"

"Sorry, Jen. Got to go."

"Millie…"

"Don't worry. I'm absolutely fine. In fact, I'm better than fine. I love you, Jen. Send my hugs and kisses to the girls and tell them I'll see them on Christmas Eve."

"I will but…"

"Bye."

She severed the connection with her bewildered sister, excitement rushing through her veins. She had no idea whether Zach had heard her conversation with Jen, unsure if she wanted him to have heard or not, but she was certain of one thing; that whatever label she chose to put on her relationship with Zach, whenever she was in his company he made her spirits soar and her self-esteem burgeon.

She smiled at him, taking in the sprinkle of debris that dotted his hair after his workshop rescue heroics, and made her way down the stairs, pausing on the bottom step so she could look directly at him. In that moment, she decided there was no time like the present to throw caution to the wind and tell Zach how she felt about him, despite their uncertain future.

"Zach..."

"Millie..."

She stared into the chocolate brown eyes, ringed with lashes the colour of liquorice, that had accompanied her dreams ever since she'd returned from St Lucia.

"Are you okay?"

For a few seconds she was unable to respond. Wisps of Zach's breath tickled seductively at her cheeks as he took a step closer, the determination evident in his expression. She savoured the swirl of pleasure that spiralled through her veins, breathless with anticipation of finally being wrapped into his arms, safe from falling roofs and the wider world. A shiver of intense desire shot southwards and her heartbeat hammered out a medley of delight as Zach's lips hovered within inches of hers. This time she knew he had no intention of backing off like he had done when they'd had dinner at his lodge, that at last the director of her destiny had answered her fervent request to give her a break!

"Never better. Zach, I want to…"

"Millie? Zach? Please tell me that wasn't an explosion I heard coming from Tim's workshop! I specifically asked him not to set foot in the damn place until this afternoon's viewing is over and Dexter and Sven have left!"

Millie took a quick step away from Zach, embarrassed to be discovered in such a compromising stance in Claudia's hallway. Unfortunately, she had forgotten she was standing on the bottom step and she stumbled forwards into Zach's arms. She almost swooned when he drew her close to his chest, enjoying the sensation of her body moulding perfectly into his, thrilled at the speed of his heartbeat through his sweater.

"Sorry, Claudia, but you're spot on," said Zach, his arm lingering on Millie's shoulder as they tipped their chins upwards in unison to watch Claudia jog down the stairs towards them, her expression a mixture of anxiety and irritation. "There's been a small incident in the workshop, nothing too serious, and Tim's fine. But you might want to add another new roof to your 'To Do' list."

"Well, I'm glad he's okay. But I need to have a word with him about concealing the damage until

Dexter has been. Do you think we should… What's the matter? Why are you looking at me like that?"

"Erm…" began Millie.

"Why don't we go through to the kitchen and grab some coffee," suggested Zach, tossing a quick glance in the direction of the library door behind which Tim, Dexter and Sven were sequestered.

"Zach? Oh, God no! Dexter's already here, isn't he?"

"Yes."

"And… oh, please don't tell me that Sven Andersen is with him?"

"I'm afraid he is."

"And I suppose they had a front row seat at the Tim Croft Crazy Circus?"

"We all did," laughed Leo, appearing at the kitchen door with Gina, Mike and Marianne, a glint of mischief in his eyes. "Had I known this kind of show was on offer right here, I might have thought twice about the entertainment I have planned for later on this evening in Oxford. You should charge extra, Claudia." Leo continued to chuckle but when he noticed the look on Claudia's face he swiftly cleared his throat and continued "Anyway, if you'll excuse us, we'll be making tracks. Don't want to miss the ice-creams!"

Millie watched them disappear through the boot room door into the courtyard and then joined Zach and Claudia at the kitchen table. Despite having spent the majority of the day resting in her bedroom, Millie still thought Claudia looked exhausted, with a tinge of green around her gills. She watched her take a sip of the coffee Zach had handed to her and screw up her nose in disgust.

"Yuk. I think there's something wrong with this batch of coffee. It tastes like liquid tar."

Millie glanced at Zach who shrugged his shoulders, took a gulp of his own, and gave Millie a slight shake of head.

"Okay. Let's get this over with," said Claudia. "Where are Dexter and Sven hiding?"

"Tim took them into the library to have a chat."

Claudia heaved herself out of her chair as if the weight of the world was on her shoulders. Millie found she had to quell the urge to offer her an arm to lean on as they made their way across the hallway towards the library. A sudden blast of concern whipped through her. Could Claudia be suffering from something other than a sickness bug?

Zach was about to open the library door when the front door burst open and a crowd of people spilled into the entrance hall, every one of them bundled up against the cold in padded jackets, and woolly hats and scarves.

"What the…?" cried Millie.

Chapter Fifteen

"Hi Claudia. The village grapevine has gone into over-drive and we thought maybe Tim could do with a hand to tidy up and mend the roof – there's more snow predicted for tomorrow night," said Mitch, the landlord of The Flying Fox, dragging his hat from his head to reveal a shock of red hair.

"Yay! The cavalry's here! Lead me to the cranberry cupcakes and hot chocolate!" declared Blake, rushing forward to draw Millie into a bear hug, crushing her face against his banana-yellow down jacket. "Better get working on the provisions for the troops."

"Hello Claudia," said Kate, as she released Zach from a hug and turned to embrace her friend. Millie cringed when she spotted the wicker basket hooked over her arm, crammed with her signature corned beef-and-potato pies and the inevitable blocks of parkin. "Hi Millie."

"Hi Kate. Erm, I..."

Millie was about to follow Kate into the kitchen when the front door was flung open a second time and, accompanied by a flurry of snowflakes, in walked another battalion of helpers swelling the numbers to over a dozen. The volume of animated chatter increased three-fold as everyone greeted everyone else, then clattered off into the kitchen for a fortifying feed before the hard work began.

The noise had alerted Tim and the door to the library cracked open. When he saw Mitch, he dashed forward, his palm outstretched, keen to lead the procession to the workshop to explain what had happened and for an in-depth discussion on how best to protect his precious collection of junk from the elements. Millie remained in the hallway, amazed at the rapid response of the call-to-arms. A warm sensation meandered through her veins until she noticed the expression of horror on Sven's face as he watched the procession of villagers trample through the hallway leaving behind trails of mud and pools of melted snow on the floor.

"Who are all these people?" demanded Sven, his mouth curled downwards in distaste.

"They're…" began Dexter, pausing to consider his response, clearly wrestling with his conscience until a black-and-white springer spaniel by the name of Binks rushed up and began circling his legs in excitement, snuffling at the pocket of his overcoat for a treat. Dexter reached down and fondled the dog's silky ears receiving a lick of approval for his effort. "They're friends. People who live in the village who have answered a fellow resident's call for support."

"Does this sort of thing happen regularly?"

"All the time."

Sven gaped in astonishment, mingled with a soupcon of fear, as a third contingent arrived on the threshold, this group accompanied by several excitable children carrying huge inflatable reindeers which they proceeded to arrange where the Christmas tree had stood. One of the men recognised Dexter and strode forward to shake his hand warmly and slap him on the back.

"The wanderer returns! Great to see you Dex. Fancy a pint in The Fox later? Reckon the drinks'll be on Tim, don't you? What's he gone and done this time?"

"Raised the roof on the workshop."

"Nothing new there then! Let's go and assess the damage!"

Dexter's friend dragged him off into the kitchen leaving Millie and Sven alone in the entrance hall. If it were possible, Sven's already translucent pallor had blanched further as he witnessed the constant stream of visitors march through Stonelea Manor as if they owned the place. However, when he reached the kitchen doorway, he stopped in his tracks at the sight of the maelstrom of chaos.

The clutter from the brunch preparations was still there, but now every available square of space was covered in coats, hats, gloves, Tupperware boxes of food, crates of beer and bottles of wine, wreaths of holly and mistletoe, and women chatting with Claudia, giggling as she regaled them with the details of another of Tim's fiascos. Millie couldn't help but smile, because there was no sign of the earlier tiredness as Claudia stood amongst her friends and laughed with them about her husband's foibles.

Without thinking, Millie turned to comment about the fabulousness of friends, about how life was enriched by their uplifting presence, no matter how fleeting, but Sven's mask of arrogance had slipped to be replaced with a look of absolute discomfort, which morphed swiftly into panic. She watched him remove his hand sanitiser and squirt a generous dollop into the palm of his hand, and then flick his eyes towards the front door, clearly preparing to make a run for it.

Having honed her skills in prevarication over many years, Millie wondered what to do for the best. On the one hand, she didn't want to do anything to jeopardise Tim and Claudia's chance at securing a sale of the manor, but equally she knew that Sven wasn't the right person to take over its custodianship. It was none of her business really, but she also suspected that Sven wouldn't be happy there and just needed a little nudge to realise that. Should she butt out and let destiny take its course, or, as was her tendency, don her Meddlesome Millie hat?

She decided to encourage Sven to join the throng in the kitchen. The whole room was filled with a kaleidoscope of colour, of fragrances, and of people. Christmas carols blared from the radio and laughter ricocheted around the walls. No one batted an eye at the anonymous superstar in their midst and she could see the disappointment in his expression, along with the distaste at having to rub shoulders with so many strangers without the protection of an entourage. She handed him a coffee, managing to slop a couple of droplets onto his designer overcoat that he still hadn't removed. She grabbed a slice of kitchen towel and tried to blot the dribble away, knocking a packet of icing sugar onto the floor with her elbow and sending clouds of sweet white mist into the air. Sven backed away towards the entrance hall, horror scrawled across his features, and Millie had an idea.

She caught up with him at the bottom of the staircase.

"Magnificent, isn't it?"

"Yes, it's a real work of art; one that should be in a museum. I plan to replace it with a glass and

stainless-steel design, much more elegant and sophis-
ticated, don't you think, Miss Harmer?"

Millie was too appalled by his suggestion to even
pull him up for getting her name wrong. She now
had no qualms about putting her plan into action. She
just hoped that Claudia and Tim would forgive her.
Surely they would be horrified too when they heard
about Sven's intentions to rip out the staircase that
had adorned Stonelea Manor for over two hundred
years. It would be tantamount to assault!

"You know, Claudia and Tim hold annual Banister
Sliding competitions for the village children. It's one
of the highlights of the local primary school's calendar
and there's a prize for the fastest. There's even a silver
trophy that's presented by the head of the household."

"Really?"

Millie was gratified to hear the slight wobble in
Sven's high-pitched voice. She wasn't sure, but she
thought she could also see beads of sweat gathering
along his upper lip as he continued to sidle towards
the front door. She had no intention of letting him
escape so easily.

"It's a shame you weren't here on Sunday to attend
the tree-lighting ceremony."

"The tree-lighting ceremony?"

"Yes, that would be another of your delightful
duties as owner of Stonelea Manor. Afterwards,

everyone piles back here for a sumptuous buffet and as much mulled wine as you could swim in. There are party games, drinking competitions, Christmas Karaoke and at the end of the evening everyone dances the Conga through the house and grounds."

"The Conga?" Sven's features twisted into a knot of disgust. "Oh, well, thanks for the information, Martha. Actually, I've just remembered an important…"

"But you haven't had a tour of upstairs yet."

"No, I'm sure it…"

"We have guests staying at the moment – I think you met Leo and Mike earlier, just before the explosion – but I'm happy to show you my suite so you can get an idea of the quality of the accommodation."

Without waiting for his approval, Millie jogged up the stairs and waited for Sven to join her with a beaming smile. She turned the iron key in the lock on her bedroom door and welcomed him into the tropical paradise with a flourish of her hand. It took all her willpower not to laugh out loud as he performed a comedic double-take when his eyes fell on the assortment of snow globes on the mantlepiece – not to mention the exotic birds, flowers and plants depicted on the wallpaper and the soft furnishings. It looked like the tropical birdhouse at a Caribbean zoo, minus the smell.

"What do you think? Marvellous, isn't it?"

"It's certainly unique."

Sven ran his fingers through his bleached blonde spikes and rotated his gaze around the room, taking in the cornucopia of zinging colours and the rainbow of matching accessories, lingering for several minutes on the disaster that was the Christmas tree, entwined with every shade of tinsel available in Gloucestershire. Coupled with the Oriental rug and her discarded clothes, the place was a riot of disorder and as far from the clean lines and minimalist Scandinavian design that Sven preferred as you could get – and Millie loved it.

"Erm, are all the rooms like this?"

Millie thought of the tastefully decorated suites Claudia had spent a fortune on; in lemon, aquamarine, the palest of lavender, all adorned with beautiful furnishings and designer linen, and she decided to embroider the truth with a little mischief.

"Oh no."

"Thank God!"

"All the suites have different themes. There's the Egyptian Suite, with hieroglyphics etched onto the walls and the ceiling and stitched into the soft furnishings. But the crowning glory is the replica of Tutankhamun's tomb that you walk through to get to the bathroom. It's fabulous!"

"Tutankhamun's tomb?" Sven spluttered, and to Millie's amazement he removed a large mono-grammed handkerchief and actually mopped his brow. A spasm of sympathy shot into her chest and she wondered if she had maybe gone a little bit too far, until he said "I had no idea the celebrated Claudia Croft had such diabolical taste in interior design! She's married to a highly-regarded architect, for God's sake!"

It took every ounce of Millie's self-control not to bite his head off. How dare he?

"And why on earth do Claudia and Tim put up with this disgraceful invasion of their home? Do these people have no respect for their privacy? If this was my property, I'd install a state-of-the-art electric gate system, so that visitors would have to announce themselves and I could decide whether I wanted them to grace me with their presence. Tell me, is there just the one access road in, do you know?"

"There're several entrances, but I don't think any of them are electric."

"So, no electrified fences either?"

Millie glanced at him sharply, expecting to see the hint of a joke in his vivid blue eyes, but to her amaze-ment it seemed he was being serious. She redoubled her efforts.

"No, but there're the tunnels that lead from the cellar to the village pub."

"Tunnels?

"Really handy for when it's snowing, or when the manor is cut off during the floods."

"The floods? Is the property prone to flooding? Dexter didn't mention that in his sales pitch. I can't live somewhere where there's a risk I could be trapped. I often have important business to attend to...."

Sven met Millie's eyes and she returned his steady stare, praying that he hadn't rumbled her attempt to thwart his impression of the manor's attributes. Fortunately, he showed no inkling of suspecting her of being parsimonious with the truth and she suspected that as far as Sven was concerned, he had long since donated his sense of humour to a worthier cause. Suddenly, she didn't want to be in his company for a moment longer and craved the opportunity to mingle with the hordes downstairs, to feel the warmth and companionship of the people who had turned up at Stonelea Manor to offer their help. She couldn't get out of her bedroom fast enough.

"Well, if you've seen everything you need...?"

"More than enough. In fact...."

Sven almost galloped down the staircase, calling a last instruction over his shoulder.

"Martha, would you tell Dexter I had an urgent business call, please?"

"It's Millie…"

But he ignored her correction and sprinted out of the front door, down the steps and jumped into his Porsche Cayenne, shooting down the driveway like Lewis Hamilton's older brother.

"Was that Sven?" asked Dexter, coming to stand next to her on the front steps, his hands shoved into his pockets as he watched the vehicle's red tail lights disappear through the stone pillars.

"Yes. I don't think he's coming back, sorry."

"Don't be. He was one of the most unpleasant men I've ever had the displeasure of dealing with. You should have heard his spiel as we drove over here. If my mother hadn't brought me up with impeccable manners, I would have ditched him at the side of the road on our way out of Oxford. There's no way I want him as the manor's new owner, even if it does mean I'll be foraging in the hedgerows for my own food for a while. I've done some crazy things in my life, but I think this has been one of the worst. How could I have forgotten how wonderful the Berryford villagers are and how central the manor is to the local community! Now, if you'll excuse me, I have some apologising to do to Claudia… but not before I challenge you to a race down the banister, Miss

Harper. And by the way, I loved the idea of an annual competition," he smirked.

"What... You heard?"

"Every word! Bravo! I might hire your services when I'm in need of a PR ninja!"

"Actually, my dream job is to be a cookery school presenter, like Claudia."

"You never know, there could be an opening here at the Cotswold Cookery School."

Millie watched Dexter bound up the stairs two at a time and then turn back to face her, his eyebrows raised.

"Scared?"

Millie giggled. "No way!" She sprinted after him, cocked her leg over the banister, leaned forward, and readied herself for the thrill she hadn't expected to repeat.

"On three! One... two... three!"

This time Millie let go immediately and shot down the polished handrail at speed, grateful that she was wearing slinky trousers that gave her the slight edge over Dexter's dress pants. She beat him by a couple of seconds and they both ended up in a pile on the floor, laughing like a pair of naughty toddlers.

"Hurray! Manic Millie is back!" smirked Zach, appearing seemingly out of nowhere to reach down to help her up.

"Don't know if that's the right description for your girlfriend, Zach. I think she should be rechristened Marvellous Millie because she's just managed to hustle Sven from the premises without a rude word in sight!"

Chapter Sixteen

"Okay, Tim, I think that should hold things until you've had chance to call out a roofer," said Mitch, wiping his hands on a cloth and shoving it back into his jacket pocket. The men shook hands before Tim pulled the landlord of The Flying Fox into a grateful hug. "Everyone's retired to the pub for a drink. You're welcome to join us?"

"Thanks, Mitch, you're a star. I'm not sure we'll make it so would you open a tab for me and remind everyone they're invited to the drinks party tomorrow night? Seven p.m. sharp."

"Sure."

"And I promise the place will be screaming Christmas festivities! What do you think, Claudie?"

"Absolutely, darling! Decorations galore!"

Tim's eyes softened as he looked at his wife, his tiredness evident from the drop of his shoulders and the smudges of grey beneath his eyes. He was covered from head-to-toe in a layer of dust and what looked like a smear of chocolate on his cheek but was probably engine oil, and Millie had to suppress a giggle.

"Bye, Claudia, thanks for the coffee and the Christmas pastries. Might see you later, Zach? Millie?"

Millie would have loved to have trotted down to the village pub for a drink, but she didn't think she could remain upright for another minute. She had been on her feet since six a.m. that morning, had prepared and presented the Festive Feast brunch tutorial, then dealt with the surprise arrival of Dexter and Sven, assisted in the continual supply of coffee, hot chocolate and warm mince pies, Stollen, Panettone, and slabs of Kate's parkin to Tim's workshop. Next, she had got cracking with the tidying up which was desperately overdue; washing and drying the glasses and plates, wiping down the worktops and polishing the floor until it gleamed. Claudia had made a valiant effort to handle the mop but had only got a quarter of the way round when she had turned a sickly yellow colour and slumped into a waiting chair, filled with apologies.

However, Millie had encountered busier days at Étienne's and she realise that her exhaustion was as a result of her churning emotions. For the last two hours she had been treated as one of the villagers; no longer a passing stranger, but an integral part of the community of Berryford and she loved it.

Through the kitchen window, she watched Mitch round up the last of the stragglers, bundle them into his truck, and zoom away down the driveway. For a couple of wonderful seconds the room was plunged into silence.

"Claudia, I need to..." began Dexter, a wobble evident in his voice.

"Why don't we retire into the library for a nightcap," suggested Tim. "Millie, Zach, could you join us, please?"

Millie glanced at Zach who gave her one of his signature smirks, shrugged his shoulders and accompanied her to the cosy, book lover's paradise where the fire glowed with the final embers of the day. Tim chose his favourite wrinkled leather chair and Claudia perched on an upholstered footstool next to him, resting her head on his arm.

A squirm of awkwardness meandered through Millie as she and Zach took the Chesterfield, leaving Dexter to sit in the wing-backed armchair, his head lowered, his hands clasped between his knees, studiously avoiding everyone's gaze. Millie could see he was desperate to explain himself and to make amends for the mistake he had made. However, she also thought that this was a family discussion that she and Zach should have no part of. Okay, Sven had backed out of the transaction, but the manor's narrow escape from becoming an Ikea in the Cotswolds was merely a temporary reprieve.

To break the impasse, Zach stepped in to perform the role of host and handed everyone a glass of Cognac. Millie took a sip and enjoyed the way the liquor scorched its way down her throat sending spasms of warmth tingling into her fingertips. She relaxed, leaned back in her seat and waited for Tim to launch into whatever it was he wanted to say.

"First of all, I want to thank Zach and Dexter for helping with the workshop roof. Without your help my precious belongings would never have survived the winter. Millie, Claudie, you've done an amazing job of keeping everyone's spirits up by providing a stream of delicious Christmas goodies, so thank you too."

Tim paused to drop a kiss on Claudia's head and take a sip of his brandy.

"Dexter…"

"No, Tim, I want to speak first."

At last Dexter raised his head, pushed his glasses up to the bridge of his nose and met Claudia's gaze. "I owe everyone an apology for the way I've conducted myself these last few months. I've caused unimaginable heartache by my actions. How could I have forgotten what the manor means to the community? It's just amazing how everyone has rallied around to help in your hour of need. I miss that. I'm sorry."

"Thank you, Dexter."

"What I can't forgive myself for is forgetting how much this place means to you, Claudia. It's not only your place of business – the fabulous cookery school which I know you love - it's your home and if someone had tried to take my home away from me, I would have been devastated, but also extremely angry. Since my parents died, you've both been nothing but kind to me and I've repaid you in the worst way possible. All I can do is beg your forgiveness and promise you that I've learned an important lesson today. It's no one else's fault but my own that the bank is calling in the loan. I made some rash decisions, but they should never have impacted on you, Claudia, and what you've achieved here."

Dexter took a gulp of his brandy and watched the flames dance in the grate for a few beats.

"Dex…"

"No, Claudia, please. I don't deserve your words of understanding. I'm flying back to Australia on Saturday and I intend to sell up. It won't cover what I owe, but it'll give me some breathing space. I'm coming back to live in the UK. I'll get a proper job and I can promise you that my days of speculating are well and truly over."

"Dex, Tim and I will help you out financially, if we can."

"No. I made this mess and it's me who should sort it out. I can't believe I even contemplated showing Sven this place. What was I thinking? He has no concept of what owning a property in the English countryside means. When I heard what he had planned for the staircase, well, if Millie hadn't stepped in when she did I think I would have doffed him over the head with a one of your walking sticks!"

All eyes swung to Millie and heat flushed into her cheeks. At Dexter's insistence she told them about Sven's proposed steel and glasses staircase, and his plans to electrify the boundary fences, and everyone gasped.

"Actually, I have Millie to thank for everything really."

"What do you mean?" asked Zach, sitting up straighter, his eyes resting on hers with such intensity she had to look away.

"As you have gathered, Sven prefers a minimalist look when it comes to interior design projects. On the drive over here, he waxed lyrical about how his numerous homes in Sweden boast cutting-edge architectural design. No visible electrical appliances, smooth, glossy surfaces, no soft furnishings and not a picture frame in sight; in effect, a clinical white box in which to spend what little spare time he has. Not my idea of a welcoming home, but each to their own."

"What's that got to do with Millie?" asked Zach, his smirk causing his dimples to appear. "If anything, she is the complete opposite. A fully paid-up member of the clutter and mess brigade and as far away from Sven on the spectrum of orderliness as it's possible to get."

"Exactly! Claudia, you weren't here when we arrived. You should have seen the look on Sven's face when he saw the state of the kitchen."

"What do you mean the state of the kitchen?"

A swirl of remorse spun through Millie's chest and she cast a swift glance at Tim who chuckled with delight. "Erm, yes, actually, I think I need to take the credit for half of that. I offered to help Millie out with this morning's tutorial as sous chef. I had the best fun outside of my workshop, but I don't think I'm going to be stepping in your shoes any time soon, darling. I'm afraid to say that by the time we'd finished eating brunch the place was, well, a little untidy."

"Untidy? It looked like the Cotswolds Culinary Massacre!" declared Dexter, warming to his subject, his head raising as he realised he had been forgiven for his slip in integrity. "Sven was horrified, and I think that spelled the beginning of his escape back to civilisation. He had only seen the house from the photographs I'd sent him and, as they were the promotional ones Claudia uses to publicise the cookery courses, they are pretty stunning."

"You mean Sven couldn't look past a little bit of clutter?" asked Claudia.

"Oh, I'm sure he was able to do that. No, that was just the prologue to the horror story that was about to unfold for the addict of symmetry and uniformity. That's where Millie came in."

"How?"

As Dexter relayed the conversation in graphic detail, embroidered with a few embellishments, Millie waited for Claudia and Tim's reaction with dread. She knew she shouldn't have interfered in something that had nothing to do with her and she felt awful. It was her turn to grasp the apology baton.

"I'm…"

"Oh my God, Millie. Thank you! Thank you!" Claudia leapt from her seat and pulled Millie into her arms, the tears glistening at her lashes golden as they reflected the firelight.

"So, let me get this right. Are you actually telling us that Millie's tendency to disperse disorder wherever she goes saved the manor from a fate worse than demolition?" asked Zach, his eyes widened as he scratched his chin in disbelief.

"That's exactly what I'm saying, and if you don't mind, Millie, I'd also like to offer you a hug for what you've done to bring me to my senses – something I should have done much sooner."

A surge of emotion reared up in her chest as she accepted Dexter's embrace, and then a pat on the back from Tim who had been moved to an emotional silence.

"Oh my God! I'll never hear the last of it!" said Zach, dropping his face into his hands. But Millie saw the gleam of happiness in his eyes, coupled with the ubiquitous glint of mischief. "I don't care what Dexter says, I'm still not letting you loose in my kitchen!"

Chapter Seventeen

Friday dawned with a wide canopy of brilliant blue sky and freezing temperatures. The sun poked its face above the treetops, the air fresh, crisp and exhilarating. From where Millie lingered in the warmth of her duvet she had a wonderful view of Stonelea's grounds and she was forced to smile when she saw a robin sitting on the windowsill watching her. She took it as a good omen and wondered what the last day of the Festive Feast cookery course would have in store.

With a spurt of energy, she jumped into the shower. Memories of the previous evening rushed back at her; the declaration made by Dexter that she had single-handedly saved the manor – for the time being at least – and the warmth of Claudia and Tim's embrace when they had eventually said good night and climbed the stairs to bed. Zach had relaxed too, knowing that his position as estate manager was secure, and she experienced a nip of pleasure as she recalled the way they had lingered at the boot room door the previous evening.

"What a day!" she'd declared, turning to meet Zach's eyes with a smile.

"You can say that again. Tell me, is every day like this in your world? Because it seems that ever since I rescued you from that puddle in St Lucia, my life has been turned into a whirlwind of confusion, calamity and nervous expectation for the next bout of chaos." Then he'd leaned forward to stroke a wisp of hair from her face and his voice had softened. "There's never a dull moment when you're around, Millie Harper; every second is crammed full of adventure."

For once, Zach's familiar twist of mischief had been absent. The intensity of his gaze told Millie everything she needed to know, and desire had scorched around her body erasing the final kernel of doubt she'd harboured about his feelings for her since arriving at Stonelea Manor.

"I've got you to thank for that, Zach," she'd whispered, her heart beating out a concerto of elation. "You've shown me how to *be* adventurous; how to find the courage to fly through the air with abandon on a zip wire or on the back of a snowmobile; how to take the time to savour the sights, sounds and smells of the tropical rainforest or English country-side, not forgetting how to appreciate the flavours of an exotic Caribbean cocktail or a spiced Christmas punch! Being with you makes all my senses zing! But, the best thing of all is that you've helped me to understand how important it is to squeeze every ounce of excitement out of life!"

The tremble in her voice had matched the wild vibration of emotion that zipped through her body, but she needed to continue, to make sure that Zach understood how she felt about him, how much their relationship meant to her, that she had fallen in love with him.

"Meeting you has transformed my view of the future from monochrome to glorious technicolor, and I… and I…"

Words had failed her at the last minute, so she'd decided to show Zach what she meant by taking a step forward, snaking her arms around his neck, and pressing her body against his. She'd had no need of the emergency sprig of mistletoe secreted in her pocket as Poppy had recommended, because Zach had lowered his mouth to hers and kissed her with such unbridled passion that her knees had weakened. She'd responded with delight, her pulse dancing the Tango as excitement coursed through her veins.

Her lips still tingled with the thought of it!

And who knew how the night might have ended had Dexter not, with spectacularly bad timing, appeared in the kitchen and steadfastly insisted on preparing himself a cup of coffee, chatting to them animatedly throughout, oblivious to the deathly glare Millie was giving him. Sadly, Dexter had not taken the hint before Leo and his friends barged in, searching for a midnight snack, singing the praises of the pantomime, even performing an impromptu rendition of the chorus much to Gina's amusement.

As she rinsed the shampoo from her eyes, she considered her and Zach's chequered history in the path of romance. Now that she understood why he had backed off from kissing her after their dinner at his lodge, his consideration for her wellbeing made her heart perform a delicious somersault and her feelings for him blossomed still further. Poppy had been right – he hadn't wanted to start a new relationship when he knew he was leaving in January; it would have been too difficult for both of them after what had happened with Chloe and Luke – better they remain friends than become lovers. Fortunately, that argument no longer held sway!

She dried her hair and ran a dollop of coconut oil from root to tip, the fragrance sending her thoughts back to the sun-filled times she and Zach had enjoyed in St Lucia. Whenever she thought of the villa perched on the hill overlooking Soufrière and the Pitons, her lips curled into a smile. She had somehow felt freer, lighter, more joyful when she was there – even during the daily deluge of liquid sunshine as her taxi driver Clavie had labelled the regular tropical rainstorms.

However, despite the natural paradise she had encountered, even the friendships of Ella and Lottie, Dylan and Henri, and the fabulous Paradise Cookery School itself, she had to admit that the icing on the cake had been Zach Barker and his quirky line in wit and sarcasm with which to jolt her from her melancholy over the ending of her relationship with Luke. She was happier than she had ever been and that was solely down to him - and now it seemed there was a possibility they could spend some time together and see where that might lead.

A colony of butterflies took up residence in her stomach as she skipped down the stairs to grab her first coffee of the day. She had expected to see Claudia there, but remembered that Tim had insisted on making a doctor's appointment for her that morning and they must have already left. She knew it would be a couple of hours at least before Leo and Gina, Mike and Marianne surfaced because the demonstration of festive canapés wasn't scheduled until two o'clock.

She grabbed a croissant and made a start on the ingredients required to prepare the menu for that evening's party. Tim was in charge of the drinks and

Mitch had promised a barrel of his best craft ale, a vat of spice-infused mulled wine, and his famous Christmas punch which according to Zach was like paint stripper and to be avoided at all costs. She decided to take his advice because her train back to London was booked for the following afternoon and she didn't want to spoil her last day at Stonelea suffering from a hangover. She couldn't believe she had only been in Berryford for a week. She felt as though she had been there for years. She had been welcomed and accepted as part of the community and that filled her with warmth and a whole host of Christmas joy.

When at last Millie paused to survey the kitchen, a surge of satisfaction rolled through her body. Six sets of ingredients were in bowls covered in clingfilm and lined up on each workstation ready for the afternoon's demonstration. Every work surface sparkled under the overhead lights and all the equipment she had used was back where it belonged. It was a real achievement and one which, surprisingly, she hadn't found too onerous. Poppy would be proud of her and she took a quick snap to send to her.

She checked the time and was shocked to see it was already midday. Should she take a walk down to Zach's lodge and confess her feelings before things got hectic, or should she wait until after the drinks reception? Or would it be better to do it the next day when they could spend the time together without interruption?

She decided that in affairs of the heart there was no time like the present. She washed her hands, tossed her apron to one side – well, it was a journey not a destination! – and made for the boot room.

"Oh, hi Tim!"

"Hello, Millie.

Tim pushed past her, wrestling with an enormous Christmas tree which he deposited in the entrance hall, wiping the perspiration from his brow with the back of his hand. Zach followed with another two fragrant fir trees, one under each arm, and set about putting one up in the library and the other in the dining room.

"The decorations are in boxes under the stairs, Millie. If you've finished the preparations for the Festive Feast demonstrations this afternoon, wouldn't mind a bit of help to turn this place into the best Christmas grotto this side of Oxford?"

"Sure. Where's Claudia?"

"Stayed on in town to do a bit of last minute Christmas shopping."

"Oh."

Millie glanced at Tim's face and saw a wide beaming smile, his cheeks splashed with circles of red, his eyes dancing with excitement. She wanted to ask why Claudia had decided to stay in Berryford when they had the presentation to deliver in forty minutes but decided against it. However, the jollity in Tim's demeanour told her something had happened that morning, or maybe it was just the reprieve from the worry of the manor's future and he was determined to celebrate.

"Tim, is everything..."

"Never better, Millie, never better." And to her amazement he hugged her, managing to stab her cheek with a sprig of holly in the process. "Ooops, sorry!"

"Tim? Where do you want me to put this garland?" asked Zach, traipsing through her pristine kitchen with his muddy boots carrying a long necklace of interwoven greenery, pine cones, ribbons and baubles.

"Mantlepiece in the library, please. Could you help Millie with the mistletoe for the doorways?"

"Absolutely!"

Millie saw Zach glance across at her, his eyebrows raised suggestively until his eyes fell on the work surfaces in the kitchen and a smile split his cheeks.

"Did you do the preparations this morning?"

"I did."

"Looks great."

Zach waited until Tim had disappeared into the dining room and moved closer to her, so close the aroma of his cologne tickled at her nostrils sending her emotions into turmoil. If she hadn't known before, her body was certainly screaming its desire at her now. It was the perfect time to tell him how she felt.

"Zach…"

"Millie…"

"You go…"

Her mouth was inches from his, her heart beating out a concerto of jubilation. No sooner had their lips met than there was a triumphant exclamation from the hallway.

"Oh my God! Oh my God! Oh my God! Are you serious?"

Millie rolled her eyes and Zach whispered, "Later. Better go and see what's bothering Tim."

They rushed into the entrance hall to see Tim standing stock-still with his mobile phone pressed to his ear, his mouth gaping and his face as red as the Santa's hat dangling from his hands.

"Everything okay?"

"Okay?" Tim repeated, staring at them as if they were strangers.

Millie giggled.

"Oh, yes, erm, that was Claudia. I…"

He stopped, his eyes fixed unseeingly on the oil painting hanging next to the library door.

"Tim?"

"Yes, sorry. Yes. Well, they do say good news comes in threes."

Again a pause.

"Tim!" cried Millie and Zach in unison.

"Yes, that was Claudia. She's just had a call from Giles, her agent, about the Caribbean cookery book idea. Apparently, quite a few publishers loved his pitch yesterday and there was a very exciting auction for the rights. But the best bit is…"

Millie saw Tim's Adam's apple working overtime as he fought the sudden sweep of emotions.

"Yes?"

"The best bit is he's also negotiated a TV show tie-in with Claudia showcasing everything the Caribbean has to offer, ably assisted by Ella of course, so with that in the pipeline, and a very decent advance for the book, it means… it means…"

Tim was unable to continue and sat down with a bump on the bottom step, a string of fairy lights looped around his neck like a Hawaiian lei.

"…it means we'll be able to raise the money to buy Dexter's share of the manor. The cookery school is safe!"

Millie scooted to his side and flung her arms around his shoulders. She knew tears were glistening at her eyelashes, but when she glanced up at Zach she didn't see the eye roll she had expected but an intense happiness scrawled across his handsome features. She hadn't yet had the chance to tell him how she felt about him but she had no doubt whatsoever in her mind that he felt the same way. It was as if, in that moment, there was an invisible connection that drew him to her, sending coils of hot desire through her whole body. She wondered what Tim would say if she launched herself at Zach and kissed him until she was breathless.

"Did I hear my name?" asked Dexter, jogging down the stairs to join them.

Tim managed to collect his thoughts, inhale a long, revitalising breath, and relay to Dexter the good news. Dexter stared at them until he succumbed to a whoosh of emotion and grabbed them one-by-one into a forceful hug.

Ten minutes later, Millie had switched on the radio and they danced to Christmas tunes while they decked the hallway with boughs of holly garlands, strings of festive bunting and every last bauble and ornament stashed in the boxes that had been hidden from view under the stairs. Even Zach got stuck in, reigning in his grumbles about untidiness and clutter with minimum effort. When they had finished, with some additional help from Leo and Gina, the whole manor was festooned in its party best for that evening's celebrations.

"Okay, we'd better get started on the food," said Millie. "Tim, have you heard from Claudia? It's two thirty and we should have started the tutorial half an hour ago."

Millie saw a flash of something indecipherable scoot across his expression and concern spread through her chest causing her stomach to squeeze uncomfortably.

"Was everything okay… this morning?" She didn't want to pry, but she needed to know that the doctor's appointment had been routine. "At the doctors?"

"All's well!" Tim declared, turning his back so she couldn't see his face and all but skipping from the room towards his beloved workshop.

Millie smiled as she took up her place behind the culinary lectern to face her eager students. She proceeded to deliver one of her best presentations ever – even if she did say so herself. By the time the last tray of mini onion bajis and sweet mince samosas were removed from the oven, and they had arranged them on Claudia's best china platters, it was after six o'clock and everyone disappeared to get ready for the celebration of the end of the Festive Feast cookery course. Knowing it would not be the last one filled Millie with a surge of elation and she couldn't wait to change into her party dress.

It had been an eventful afternoon, but that was nothing compared to how Millie's stay at Stonelea Manor had changed her. Six months ago, she would never have believed that she was ready to open up her heart and let someone in and she sent up a prayer of gratitude to the director of her destiny for their skill in story development. It had been a rocky journey with many twists and turns along the way, but one which had enabled her to grow as a person, to expand her skills as a chef, but most important of all, to fall in love.

Chapter Eighteen

Millie had never felt more glamorous. When she returned to her suite she discovered the most exquisite dress hanging on the front of her wardrobe, a pale shell–pink chiffon column, glistening with sparkles, that clung to her curves like a second skin. She had received a text from Claudia telling her it was their gift to her to express their heartfelt thanks for all her hard work and the support she had provided during the most difficult few months of Claudia's life.

Whilst she loved the dress and appreciated the gesture – she did think it rather strange that Claudia had sent her a text rather than presenting her with the gift in person so she could thank her immediately. A niggle of concern scratched at her chest, but she shoved it away, chastising herself for always reading too much into things, and concentrated on her mounting excitement for the evening ahead.

Leo and Gina had presented her with a bottle of her favourite perfume, and Mike and Marianne had given her a gorgeous diamanté hair slide which she slotted into her curls to complete her outfit. She felt like a princess going to her first ball and she recalled her conversation with Zach earlier on in the week when she had told him that her childhood dream had been to be a princess – little had she known it would come true, which was something else she had to thank him for.

She made sure she was in the kitchen fifteen minutes before the first guests were due to arrive, ready to help with the food and drink, only to discover that Claudia and Tim had engaged Mitch's teenage daughter, Erin, and five of her friends to perform waitressing duties that evening and all she had to do was relax and enjoy the celebrations.

The manor was at its most spectacular, with white fairy lights twinkling around every window and doorway, luxurious garlands of tinsel entwined around the banister, and a pair of Christmas trees standing guard at the front door. Outside, the snow-covered lawn glistened under the moonlight like a gem-encrusted blanket, dotted with golden spools of light from the lampposts that meandered down the driveway.

Millie sauntered towards the library where the rumble of conversation grew louder as the drinks flowed in abundance, all to the backing track of Christmas carols and the crackling of the logs on the fire. The fragrance of pine needles, mingled with expensive perfumes and colognes, suffused the air and her spirits edged up a notch.

Tim looked splendid in a burgundy velvet jacket and jaunty cravat, regaling his audience with the finer details of his newest invention, his face alight with animation and not a trace of his earlier tiredness. There was no sign of Claudia. Millie assumed that she was still getting ready and, as their hostess, wanted to make a grand entrance when everyone had arrived. Leo and the Festive Feast gang had dressed for the occasion in designer eveningwear and were busy quaffing cocktails mixed by a loose-wristed Mitch.

A waft of fresh air on the back of her neck told her that the front door had opened and she returned to the hallway to see if Zach had arrived. It wasn't him but the last of the guests from the village, two of whom made their way into the kitchen to deliver a contribution to the food. Kate held a huge Tupperware box aloft, topped with a chocolate yule log covered in thick dark buttercream with the most incongruous stuffed robin perched on the top. She spotted Blake too, resplendent in a bright orange shirt, black tie and matching trousers, his hair teased into a trendy quiff and a smattering of designer stubble on his jaw.

"Darling! You look a-ma-zing! That dress is sooo gorgeous! Save a dance for me later, won't you? If you can bear to tear yourself away from our gorgeous Zach, of course." Blake dragged her into a warm embrace, engulfing her in a cloud of cologne so potent that it would be enough to awake anyone's maiden aunt from the deepest of slumbers!

Millie felt warmth surge into her cheeks as at last her eyes landed on Zach, who had just that moment walked through the door. When he met her gaze, the corners of his lips turned into a smile, and her whole body tingled with anticipation. Blake released her swiftly from his hug and shot over to Zach, enveloping him too, before giving Millie a cheeky wink of encouragement, linking his arm through Kate's and escorting her towards the library.

"You look stunning!" Zach reached for her hand and wove his fingers through hers. "Come on."

With her heart fluttering against her ribcage, she floated at his side. However, Zach didn't lead her towards the melee in the library but to the boot room where he pulled her into his arms and kissed her, slowly, gently, tentatively at first, then with growing urgency until a crescendo of desire whipped around her body. She kissed him back, relishing the sensations zinging through her body, not wanting their embrace to end.

"I can't tell you how much I've wanted to do that!"

"Me too," she laughed.

Zach held her gaze for what seemed like an eternity and she melted once again into his arms, marvelling at the way her body fit perfectly against his. An avalanche of emotion surged from her stomach to her chest, and she had never been more certain of anything in her life. Her feelings for Zach had ballooned into something amazing and she wanted him to know.

"Zach, I…"

"Hey, so this is where you two are hiding," chuckled Dexter, totally oblivious to what he was interrupting. "Thought you might like to know that our hostess is about to make her entrance."

Millie giggled at the expression on Zach's handsome face. For a moment she thought he was going to refuse to leave the shadowy confines of the boot room, but of course he didn't. He hooked his arm around her waist and together they made their way to the bottom of the stairs where all the guests had congregated to await the arrival of Claudia.

A gasp of appreciation echoed around the entrance hall and Millie's spirits soared when her friend appeared at the top of the staircase looking every inch the celebrated chef she was. Claudia radiated happiness and appeared to have conquered her previous battle with exhaustion. As she lingered beneath the chandelier, her gem-encrusted gown shone like a Fabergé creation and she looked like a movie star about to accept an Oscar. Her gold-streaked hair had been professionally coiffed into a smooth glossy bob and she wore a pair of long diamanté earrings that almost brushed her naked shoulders.

Tim skipped up the steps to accompany his wife down the stairs to greet her guests – except they unexpectedly paused on the last step and waited until everyone was quiet. Millie glanced at Zach, a question in her eyes. Zach shook his head, his brow knitted slightly as he pulled her closer and dropped a kiss on the top of her head.

"Ladies and gentlemen. Claudia and I would like to thank you all for joining us this evening for the annual celebration of the end of the Festive Feast cookery course. We want you to know that we appreciate everything each and every one of you has done to support us at Stonelea Manor and at the cookery school throughout the year and this is our chance to say a huge, heartfelt thank you. As some of you know, this year has presented a number of challenges and we could not have weathered the storm without the knowledge that our Berryford family was cheering us along from the side-lines. So, before we indulge in a few glasses of Mitch's excellent Christmas punch and we forget our names – taxis will be available at midnight by the way – I'd like to make a couple of announcements."

The ripple of laughter that had reverberated around the oak-panelled hallway at the mention of Mitch's lethal punch and cocktails ceased and everyone fell silent, eager to hear what Tim was about to say.

"First of all, a piece of news that I know many of you will enjoy. We have this year's winners of the Festive Feast dessert recipes competition with us tonight, so I wanted to announce that these wonderful traditional family recipes will form part of a hand-illustrated cookery book that will be published next year in time for Christmas."

A whoop of celebration burst from the audience and high-pitched chatter filled the room until Zach noticed that Tim and Claudia had remained standing on the bottom step, waiting to continue, happiness shining from their faces as they smiled at each other with affection.

"Hang on, everyone. Let Tim finish."

The crowd quietened, and Millie felt Zach squeeze her hand as she scrutinised Claudia's expression for an idea of what they were about to reveal.

"As you all know, the Claudia Croft Cookery School means a great deal to us both. It's an integral part of our family and of village life and we were devastated when we thought we would have to close its doors. However, I'm delighted to reassure you that the school will continue for the foreseeable future. In fact, Claudia has a swathe of new ideas for even more exciting and exotic courses, and possibly even starting one for children during the school holidays."

Millie saw the excitement for the school's expansion reflected in Claudia's expression. But then a thought occurred to her. If Claudia had numerous new plans for the cookery school in the Cotswolds what did that mean for the Paradise Cookery School?

Oh my God! she thought, as a painful *thunk* of alarm slammed into her chest. Claudia wasn't thinking of closing it down and selling the villa, was she? That would be just too awful to contemplate. When she met Claudia's gaze, craving an immediate answer, she saw she was staring at her with an indecipherable look in her eyes, then her friend squeezed Tim's hand and stepped onto a higher step so that she could speak to her guests more easily.

"I'm so pleased everyone is here tonight to share in our celebrations. I want you to know that Tim and I are no longer relocating to the Caribbean as we intended but staying here in Berryford."

A whoop of delight erupted, and a couple of Tim's friends surged forward to offer him their palms.

Kate and Blake hugged Claudia, with Blake wiping away an errant tear with the back of his pinky finger, laughing at Mitch's eyeroll. However, Millie's stomach lurched like an out-of-control rollercoaster and her spirits crashed.

No!

Tears sprang to her eyes. She turned to look up at Zach, but saw he was still watching Claudia and Tim, waiting for an explanation. Millie was happy for Zach, of course, because their decision meant that his job as estate manager was secure for the foreseeable future, which in turn meant that she could see him regularly and they could build on their fledgling relationship. She was ecstatic at the thought, but she couldn't shift the nugget of sadness that was lodged in her gut about the demise of the Paradise Cookery School, a place she loved and somewhere that held a special place in her heart.

She thought of Ella, who had been overjoyed at being able to at last achieve her dream of becoming a cookery presenter, revelling in the opportunity to showcase her Caribbean recipes to a whole new audience. She thought of Lottie and Dylan, of Henri and Travis and Anisha, and the fact that she would probably never see them again, and her heart shrivelled a little.

It was a few seconds before she realised that Claudia was speaking again.

"...So, Tim and I are overwhelmed with gratitude that eventually, after ten years of trying, we are to become parents!"

The whole room exploded into shrieks of pleasure and well wishes. Zach released her grasp and strode towards Tim, shaking his hand before embracing Claudia. For the next few minutes, the couple were engulfed in congratulatory hugs and it was a while before Millie could reach Claudia.

"Claudia, I'm so pleased for you. Congratulations, you must be so happy."

"More than happy, Millie. We're over the moon. I confess that I never thought this day would come, but now it's here I can't stop myself from grinning like a five-year-old on Christmas morning. This is the best present I could ever have wished for."

Claudia led Millie into the kitchen where she fixed herself a glass of non-alcoholic punch, her cheeks glowing with merriment and gratitude, and no doubt a dollop of relief.

"The doctor confirmed it this morning. I'm sorry I wasn't here to do the canapé presentation, but I needed some time to myself to get my head around things, and I admit I did also indulged in a bit of a shopping frenzy. You look amazing in that dress, by the way."

"Thank you, Claudia. It's a wonderful gift. So, do you think that could be why you've been feeling so tired these last few weeks?"

"That's exactly why. Believe me, I had no idea I was pregnant. Tim and I had given up hoping to be parents and decided to make the cookery school our baby... and we will continue to do so, but here in the Cotswolds as I prepare for our new arrival."

Millie steeled herself to ask the next question, not sure she wanted to know the answer.

"What will happen to the Paradise Cookery School?"

"Yes. Tim and I have discussed that, and there's no way my doctor will allow me to fly backwards and forwards to present the courses, sadly. I intend to take his advice not to overburden myself... so..."

Millie felt tears collect along her lashes as memories cascaded through her mind of all the wonderful, sunshine-filled adventures she had experienced there. How much she truly loved the villa, with its aquamarine infinity pool, its painted veranda, and tropical gardens overlooking the spectacular Caribbean Sea. She felt like she was having to say goodbye to a beloved friend and it hurt. She was surprised its loss was affecting her so much, but she forced a smile on her face, and hugged Claudia close so she couldn't see her eyes.

"Claudia, I'm so happy for you. You absolutely deserve this, and I know that you and Tim will make fabulous parents."

"Thanks, Millie."

Claudia pulled away from Millie, holding her at arm's length to scour her face. Millie tried to look away, but wasn't able to before her emotions over-whelmed her and tears spilled down her cheeks.

"I'm sorry, Claudia. I'm happy for you and Tim, I really am. It's just I'm so upset about the Paradise Cookery School. It's an amazing place, and I think it's the perfect setting to showcase the very best recipes and ingredients the Caribbean cuisine has to offer."

"Well, I was hoping you would say that."

"What do you mean?"

Millie gazed at Claudia, her lips parted but no words ensued as her heart bashed out a cacophony of hope.

"I know Étienne will probably never forgive me for this, but I'd like you to run the Paradise Cookery School for me. We worked together, via the internet, amazingly when you were there in September and the Chocolate & Confetti course was a fabulous success. Did I tell you that Imogen and her mother have already rebooked for next September?

And we have five more courses fully booked. You know what to do, you know my recipes as well as I do… and Ella has already said yes to being your co-presenter. What do you say?"

"What do I say?"

Millie gasped. It was her dream come true. Not only was she being offered a job as a cookery course presenter, but it would be for the fabulous Claudia Croft Cookery School, in her, albeit biased, opinion the most prestigious in the world. Coupled with that, it was situated in one of the most gorgeous settings where the sun shined every day, the people were friendly and welcoming, the beach and the Purple Parrot beckoned after a long shift in the kitchen, but most of all, the food was fantastic and she had only just scraped the surface. She adored Ella, and her best friend Denise, and she had so much to learn from them she couldn't wait to get started.

She would have leapt at the chance without hesitation, except for one thing.

Zach.

Chapter Nineteen

Claudia was smiling at her, waiting for her enthusiastic acceptance of the offer of a lifetime.

"I… I'm thrilled that you think I'm capable of representing you in St Lucia, not to mention relieved that the Paradise Cookery School will not be closing its doors. I adore the plantation house, its grounds, the town of Soufrière, the Purple Parrot. I love Ella, and it would be a dream come true to work alongside her again, it's everything I could wish for."

"I'm sensing a but?"

Millie fiddled with the stem of her glass, battling her emotions as she wondered how to put them into words for Claudia when she hadn't even had chance to come to terms with them herself. So much had happened in a short space of time that her head was reeling from the turmoil and the decisions to be made.

However, her overriding emotion was the strength of the connection she had formed with Zach, and the unshakeable knowledge that he was her soulmate and she didn't want to lose him, no matter what prize she was offered. It was a huge opportunity to decline, but she knew with absolute certainty that she was doing the right thing. She only had to recall how she felt when she thought he was going to the Caribbean to know her feelings were real. She had fallen in love with him and that deserved a chance.

"I'm sorry, Claudia, but yes, there is a 'but'."

Tears trickled down her cheeks and her throat felt as though it had closed round a prickly pear. She swallowed, determined to formulate the right explanation as she owed Claudia so much.

"Zach…"

"Ah, before you go on, I think I should…"

"Hey! You two, come on, we're about to raise a toast to the best cookery school in the world!" cried Tim from the kitchen door. He paused, flicking his eyes from Claudia to Millie and back again. "Have you told her?"

"Yes. Have you told Zach?"

"Yes."

Millie raised her head from studying the contents of her glass where she'd hoped to find all the answers to her problems but had drawn a blank. Through a shimmering haze of tears, she saw Tim was beaming and cast a quick look at Claudia, and then noticed Zach standing behind Tim, also grinning.

"What's going on?" she asked, feeling like she was the only sane person in the room.

Zach strode across the kitchen, dragged her from her seat and kissed her. She ignored the satisfied smiles of Claudia and Tim, and the rest of the guests for all she knew, and kissed him back, enjoying the swirl of excitement, pleasure, and something altogether more physical as she pressed her body against Zach's muscular torso, desperate for more. After what felt like an eternity but was probably only a few seconds, she heard Mitch perform his best wolf-whistle and she pulled away, laughing, her heart soaring, knowing with utmost conviction that she had made the right decision to stay in London, in her little attic above the patisserie so that she could spend every spare moment in Zach's arms.

"Did you say yes?" he asked.

"Yes?"

"To running the Paradise Cookery School for Claudia?"

"No, I… Hang on. Why?"

"Because Tim has just told me that he wants me to relocate to that gorgeous wooden lodge over-looking the Caribbean Sea and to manage the cocoa plantation whilst you scatter all manner of culinary debris around the villa's kitchen. He has very sensibly decided that someone needs to be around to tidy up afterwards and I thought…"

"Oh my God! Oh my God! You will be in St Lucia!"

"Yes? I thought Claudia…"

"Hadn't quite got around to telling Millie that bit," said Claudia, snuggling under Tim's arm and gazing at Millie and Zach as if her heart would burst. "But I can assure you, Zach, if you need any assurance, that Millie was prepared to give up the opportunity of a lifetime to be with you."

Millie laughed as her heart burst with happiness.

"I love you, Zach! You make my life zing with excitement and joy! But there's one thing I want you to do before I agree to go to St Lucia with you."

"What's that?"

"Order in a year's supply of Marigolds!"

Everyone laughed as Zach curled his arms round her shoulders and stared into her eyes with such intensity she gasped.

"The feeling is mutual, marvellous, maddening Millie Harper!"

Their audience drifted away to give them some privacy and the rest of the evening disappeared in a whirl of congratulations, of hugs, of tears — mainly from Blake — of carol singing, and of fond farewells.

At midnight, Millie found herself strolling arm-in-arm with Zach down the driveway towards his lodge. It was cold, but she was snuggled into a warm padded jacket and had one of Tim's old hats pulled down over her ears. She looked across at the expanse of smooth white snow that had been untouched for almost a week, save for the impression of snow angels she and Zach had created which were still evident, alongside the mound of snow where she had tried to recreate a likeness of Binks.

"Come on, said Zach. "I've got something to show you. I had no idea the snow would last so long, but I'm glad it has because I want you to see this."

"See what?"

"Always the questions! Trust me."

Millie felt his hand slot into hers as if it were the most natural gesture in the world. A wriggle of excitement meandered through her stomach. She couldn't wait to fly out to St Lucia, to take her place alongside Ella behind the Paradise Cookery School's demonstration bench, and the added sprinkles on her cupcake of dreams was that Zach would be with her!

As they made their way towards the lodge, her thoughts meandered through the myriad possibilities for romantic moonlit walks along the beach at Soufrière, gossip-filled evenings with Ella and

Denise, Henri and Dylan, indulging in one of Lottie's potent cocktails, or simply sitting out on the veranda overlooking the Pitons starring up at the stars and thanking the director of her destiny for their benevolence.

She dragged herself back to the present and followed Zach through the front gate of his home, but instead of going inside as she had expected, he led her around to the back garden where she stopped in her tracks.

"Oh my God! Is that… is that…?"

"Do you like it?"

"I love it! Zach Barker, you are a man of many talents."

"Well, I have a few more up my sleeve…"

Millie laughed, but pulled her hand from Zach's to inspect his icy work of art more closely. She had wondered where he'd disappeared to when they were creating their snow sculptures. She remembered thinking it strange that he had chosen to build his snowman in his back garden, away from the viewing public, and now she knew why.

In the middle of his patio stood two snowmen; one slightly taller with a woolly bobble hat perched on his head, a carrot for a nose and two black pebbles for eyes. As it sported a bottle of antibacterial spray in one hand and a dog's lead in the other, it was obvious to any onlooker that it was supposed to be Zach. The second sculpture was smaller and wore a bright pink scarf, a pair of sparkly earrings and was festooned with tiny cocktail umbrellas – clearly a snow sculpture of Millie.

Suspended from a branch directly overhead was a sprig of mistletoe and the frozen statues were leaning towards each other, their faces touching in a depiction of a kiss. It was an amazing piece of art, but it was more than that. It was confirmation that Zach had loved her even before she had arrived in Berryford and she couldn't wait to explore his feelings further in the warmth of his lodge.

But first, she had to accept the invitation. She grabbed the mistletoe and waved it over her head, laughing with delight as Zach brought his lips to hers and wished her a Merry Christmas in the best way possible.

Acknowledgements

My first thank you has to be to my parents Hilary & Keith for buying me a boatload of books and instilling in me an enduring love of reading them. Thanks also have to go to my husband and son for their unfailing support – especially when there's no dinner on the table or fresh shirts to wear, but there's a new chapter in the current manuscript. Then there's my wonderful editors, Louise Cullen and Laura McCallen – a huge thank you for loving Millie and Zach as much as I do and for sprinkling your expertise on the story so that it sparkles. A tropical Caribbean rum cocktail to you both!

Daisy x

The Paradise Cookery School

Sunshine & Secrets
Confetti & Confusion
Mistletoe & Mystery

For more romance in a beautiful place
why not try the first in a new series by Daisy James?

Read on for chapter one of

Wedding Bells at Villa Limoncello

Chapter One

One Friday in Fulham.
Colour: Magnolia.

Izzie took a step back to cast a critical eye over the room she'd just finished styling. With the stark white walls of the newly-renovated property, and an employer who thought taupe was the ultimate in sophistication, she had done her best, but minimalism was an understatement! Her gaze fell on the beige linen curtains that matched the oatmeal cushions resting on the brown leather Chesterfield sofa and she cringed. Unfortunately, she'd forgotten to conceal her reaction from Jonti, her eagle-eyed colleague, who she could see was about to launch into another one of his eloquently crafted lectures.

'Darling, isn't it about time you chose your soft furnishings from a more vibrant part of the colour spectrum? I mean, ivory, chiffon and champagne maybe the go-to colours for a blissful wedding cere-mony in St Paul's Cathedral, but this is Fulham! Now,

I might not be a graduate of the Royal College of Art like you and Meghan, but don't you think a splash of Cambridge blue, or Venetian red, or my personal favourite, razzle dazzle rose, would spice up the ambience for potential buyers? Not to mention encourage them to fork out the exorbitant asking price our lord-and-master is demanding for this little piece of heavenly real estate.'

'I agree with Jonti,' declared Meghan, bursting through the front door with a tray of takeaway coffees and broadening the colour palette ten-fold. Izzie hadn't been expecting her best friend to arrive for at least another hour – Meghan always struggled to extract herself from the demands of her job as a window dresser at Harrods – and it was the first time in living memory she had been early for anything. She suspected foul play on Jonti's part. 'This place is snoring boring!'

'Snoring boring?'

'Yes! Dull, drab, characterless, bland…'

'Okay, okay, you've made your point,' laughed Izzie, reaching out to tweak a vase whose Chinese manufacturer had labelled 'frothy cappuccino' in the mistaken belief that an optimistic description would transform its basic shape into an upmarket work of art. 'However, I have to point out that this is Hambleton Homes' signature design.'

Of course, Jonti and Meghan were right to be disappointed with what she had created – the room was lacklustre by anyone's standards. Her professional eye told her that the beautifully apportioned property, with high ceilings, sculpted cornices, and chiselled ceiling roses that wouldn't have looked out of place in Versailles, was crying out for a magnificent crystal chandelier, and maybe even a bronze bust or marble statue or two.

'And Jonti and I have followed the brief to… the… letter!'

'That's because Darren Hambleton is a corporate dullard who wouldn't know taste if it rushed up and bit him on his Armani-clad buttocks. For God's sake, Izzie, have you forgotten that you used to own one of the most sought-after Interior Design studios in London with a client list the envy of Liberty's?'

'And what about that double-page spread in LuxeLife Magazine?' added Jonti, taking an experimental sip from his skinny latte before picking up the career-critique baton from Meghan. 'What did that feature writer with the movie-star good looks call you? You know, the one who fancied himself as the next Poldark? All tousled curls and rock-hard abs? It took all my self-control not to ask him where he'd left his scythe!'

'You mean Miles Carrington?' smirked Izzie.

'Ah, yes, Magnificent Miles. Now don't take this the wrong way, Izzie darling, but if he saw this dreary excuse for a living room he'd be forced to amend the effusive accolade he bestowed upon you from 'Isabella Jenkins, Queen of Colour' to 'Isabella Jenkins, Duchess of Dullness' otherwise he'd risk being sued for misrepresentation.'

Izzie shook her head. She'd heard Jonti and Meghan's complaints before – lots of times. But she had also learned that pleading the case for the defence would only prolong the discomfort currently swirling through her veins. There was no way she was about to admit that, uninspiring though it was, she actually preferred the predictability of Hambleton's design template because it cut down on the effort it took to be creative, something she was immensely grateful for. It was best to simply move the conversation on to the part where her friends shrugged their shoulders in resignation at another 'by-the-numbers' house staging so that they could launch into a blow-by-blow account of their forthcoming weekend shenanigans in the restaurants and nightclubs of Covent Garden.

Ignoring their raised eyebrows and exchanged glances, she began slotting the assorted accessories that made up the busy home-stager's armoury into her battered wheelie suitcase – industrial-sized scissors, Stanley knife, fishing wire, glue gun. Seeing everything returned to its allocated space helped to dissolve the anxiety that had been gnawing at her chest all afternoon. She snapped the lock shut, grabbed the handle, and made for the door, comforted by the fact that another job had been completed on time, and that she had side-stepped another lecture on the merits of her personal development strategy.

Sadly, her relief was short-lived. Jonti took her hand, guided her towards the sofa and sat down, lacing his manicured fingers through hers whilst Meghan took a seat on the footstool in front of her, flicking her pink-tipped blonde hair over her shoulder and avoiding Izzie's eyes. Izzie's stomach dropped to her Sketchers like a penny down a well. Oh God!

'Guys, I know you mean well, but can we not do this right now? Come on, it's Friday night, let's wrap things up here and I'll buy you both a drink.'

'Sorry sweetie, Meghan and I have decided that enough is enough. Now, you know I love you, don't you? You guys are the best friends a man could ask for in this crazy metropolis we call home. But it's not just the décor that needs an injection of colour, Izzie. I'm no Marc Jacobs, but where *did* you get that sweater? Your grandmother? What colour is it supposed to be? Ecru? Khaki? Dishcloth? If you loiter for too long next to those curtains over there you'll disappear! I suppose that's the point, though, isn't it? Although, how you think you can possibly blend into the background with that delightful mane of Titian curls, I don't know!'

'Hey, I happen to like this jeans-and-jumper combo. It's warm, comfortable, practical...'

'What sort of words are they? Comfortable and practical? You sound like my great-aunt Marge — except even she has been known to flirt with the cosmetic geniuses of Yardley and Revlon every once in a while! I know you favour the pale and interesting look, and I totally get why you don't want to cover up that cute smattering of freckles with a mask of heavy foundation, but a little tinted moisturiser wouldn't go amiss occasionally!'

Izzie shook her head, her lips twitching at the corners. She felt like a naughty schoolgirl called into the headteacher's office to give an account of her sartorial sins. She adored Jonti — he was far more than a fellow purveyor of all-things fabric and sequin-related. With his quirky sense of fashion, from the orange winkle-pickers to the rainbow-framed glasses that enhanced his bright blue eyes and his signature bleached blonde quiff, he exuded a sense of style she'd long since discarded to the realms of a past life.

'Okay, okay, I promise to break out the scarlet lipstick and gold-flecked mascara when we partake in our usual pint of Guinness at the Hope & Anchor tomorrow night. Happy?'

'I'm not *un*happy.'

She made to get up from the sofa but was uncere-moniously pulled back down. Clearly the lecture was not over yet. Now, it was Meghan's turn to assume the role of life coach.

'Unlike Jonti, I'm prepared to accept your new-found obsession with magnolia, your ever-lengthening 'to-do' lists, *and* your preference for hand-knitted garments that make you look like the Michelin Man, but when was the last time you ate a decent meal? Don't get me wrong, I love a round of buttered toast just as much as the next person, but not for every meal!'

'Meghan's right, darling. All that gluten is enough to make anyone's sparkle wither and die! My body is a temple and I just could not treat it with such disdain. How on earth do you manage to keep mind, body and soul together? I know you're not going to like me saying this, but I happen to think you've been looking a tiny bit peaky recently – like Eeyore's little sister at Winne-the-Pooh's going away party! I bet you're not sleeping properly either, are you?'

'I'm sleeping and eating just fine, thank you very much,' she lied, irritation beginning to poke its head above the parapet.

What did her diet have to do with anything? And so what if her sleep was frequently trampled on by the demons of the past? However, before she could express her indignation or make a humour-filled attempt to change the direction of their conversation to something less personal, Meghan was gearing up to launch her *coup de grâce*.

'And whilst we're on the subject of your love life...'

'My love life?' spluttered Izzie, feeling as though she'd just had a bucket of icy water tossed in her face.

'Yes, ever heard of it? When was the last time you had a date?'

'And don't try to fob us off with that old chestnut about still getting over Alex. It's been eighteen months since you guys split – you even like his new girlfriend, Perfect Penelope, whom I have to say is not a patch on you, darling. Did you see the cerise leopard-print heels she was wearing when we bumped into them at the Old Vic last month? So tacky! Although the same cannot be said for her delightfully fragrant brother Marcus – don't think I've seen biceps like that since I accidentally stumbled into the Fire Brigade's Boxing Club!'

'Jonti, off topic! Look, Izzie, all we're saying is why not take a leaf out of Alex's book and dip your toe into the shark-infested dating pool again? A little bit of romance is exactly what you need to unwrap that mantle of melancholy you insist on modelling whenever we go out!'

'Yes, sweetie, you need to break free of the past and get some music in your soul! Okay, lecture over, let's beat the post-work stampede and take a detour to that delightful little French bistro down the road and indulge in a bottle of fizz. My treat! I won't tell our slave driver of a boss if you don't?'

Jonti jumped up from the settee with a glint of schoolboy mischief lighting up his eyes.

'Best thing I've heard all day,' grinned Meghan, linking his arm as they made their way to the door. 'Come on, Izzie.'

Izzie heaved a sigh of relief that the sermon was over and was about to follow in their footsteps when her phone buzzed with an incoming text. She glanced at the screen and groaned. Was Darren psychic?

'Hang on – it's a text from Darren.'

'I thought he was showcasing his sporting prowess on the golf course this afternoon?'

Jonti's upper lip curled in disgust at another one of Darren's attempts to apply so-called 'progressive business practices' to Hambleton Homes' marketing strategy. Ever since Harry Hambleton, who had founded the business in the 1980s through sheer grit and determination, had given his son free reign to run the company, he'd been desperate to make his own mark. Unfortunately, dashing around town in his canary yellow Porsche, massaging egos and spouting corporate soundbites wasn't going down very well with many of their clients. Izzie knew that if Harry had any idea how Darren was conducting himself he would have ditched his extended sojourn in the Spanish sunshine and jumped on the next available flight back to London to remind his son that, in business, there was no substitution for hard work and integrity.

'He wants me to call him.'

'What now? It's five o'clock on a Friday!'

Jonti shook his head in irritation. He made no secret of his dislike of their new, fresh-from-business-school boss, although Izzie suspected it had more to do with Darren's enviable designer wardrobe and the fact that he smelled like a Parisian lady's boudoir than the new-style management techniques he had introduced to convince his father that the thousands of pounds he'd spent on his private education was money well spent.

'Why don't you and Meghan zip down to Pierre's and order the drinks. I'll catch you up in a few minutes.'

Unlike Jonti, Izzie did have some sympathy for Darren. It couldn't be easy stepping into Harry's shoes, not to mention coming to terms with his father's recent marriage to a woman the same age as Darren himself, especially after the death of his mother less than two years ago. She had personal experience of that kind of devastation and understood the impact it could have on anyone, no matter how privileged or comfortable their life was.

However, she also had a great deal of affection for Harry and was grateful to him for stepping into the breach with the offer of a position as a part-time house-stager when everything she knew and loved had crumbled around her ears. In another life, she had been commissioned by Darren's mother, Esme Hambleton, to completely refurbish their Knightsbridge townhouse after she'd read the feature in LuxeLife magazine. It was still one of the most enjoyable interior design projects she'd worked on and they had remained in touch until Esme had died suddenly, only six months later, which meant Izzie'd had two funerals to attend in the space of a few months.

'You go and grab a table, Jonti,' urged Meghan, pulling on the white denim jacket she'd hand-embroidered with crimson peacocks in preparation for the fifty-metre dash to the end of the street. 'Izzie and I will be right behind you. Shoo!'

Jonti rolled his eyes, planted noisy kisses on the two women's cheeks, and wriggled his fingertips. 'Later, peeps!' he said, as he set off down the street, a jaunty gait in his step. Izzie smiled, gratitude for his unwavering friendship encircling her heart as she turned back to Meghan.

'Okay, might as well get it over with.'

Izzie grimaced, eyeing her mobile as though it were a lethal weapon.

'Do not, under any circumstances, agree to work this weekend! I've got a hot date on Saturday night and I need you to help me with my buff-and-polish regime so that I sparkle like the diamond I am.'

'Who's the lucky man this time?' asked Izzie, knowing that Meghan fell in and out of love quicker than a Tigger does the Hokey-Kokey.

'He's a cameraman, worked on one of my brother's film shoots in the Caribbean last October. I met him again a couple of weeks ago at Suzie and Carlton's wedding – I'd forgotten he'd asked for my number. Oh, and don't get me started on the subject of my stupid, selfish brother! If Brad thinks I've got nothing else better to do than respond to his beck and call, then he's delusional as well as presumptuous!'

'What's he done this…'

'Anyway, whilst I've got you alone – you know what a huge gossip Jonti is – I've got another bit of amazing news. I only got the call this morning, and the whole thing is shrouded in absolute secrecy, but guess what? Giselle has broken her ankle and

Martha, my department manager at work, has asked me to *compère* the Fenella Fratenelli fashion show next Monday night! It's a dream come true. Oh, not the ankle thing, obviously – I've started a collection to send Giselle a huge bouquet crammed with her favourite sunflowers – but I'm hoping to show Martha that there's more to my repertoire than dressing windows. God, Izzie, I'm just so excited. I adore Fenella's paisley jumpsuits, not to mention her pink shearling biker jackets!'

Izzie smiled, her heart ballooning with pride as she watched Meghan pogo on the spot like a toddler in need of the bathroom. It had been Meghan's dream for as long as she'd known her to make the move from creating stunning, if slightly avant-garde shop windows to staging cat-walk shows. This could be her big break.

'Oh, Meghan, I'm so thrilled for you. This calls for an extra-special celebration. Look, why don't you go and join Jonti. I'll finish up here, give Darren a quick call, and join you at Pierre's in ten minutes.'

'Okay.'

Meghan flung her arms around Izzie, then skipped out of the front door, her colourful hair flowing in her wake like a Medusa on steroids. Izzie shook her head as she selected Darren's number.

'Hi Darren.'

'Yo, Isabella!'

She grimaced at the familiar greeting and the mid-Atlantic drawl he affected, another trait at odds with his father. Harry Hambleton was proud of his Yorkshire roots and held no truck with people who put on airs and graces.

'What did you want to talk to me about?'

'Well… actually…' For the first time ever, Izzie heard Darren pause to inhale a deep breath before launching into his usual diatribe of corporate clichés. Looking back, she realised that his out-of-character hesitation should have set alarm bells ringing. 'I thought… well, there's no time like the present to bite the bullet. Your time is precious, my time is precious, so I'll just launch right in, shall I?'

A wriggle of unease tickled at her abdomen. 'What's going on, Darren?'

'So, as managing director of HH I've been doing a bit of blue sky thinking recently and it's time to raise the bar on everything we've been doing. I'm not sure if you've noticed but we're slap bang in the middle of an economic hurricane, so it's imperative that we push the envelope to come up with new and dynamic ways to eliminate waste and maximise profit. It's all about the bottom line, wouldn't you agree, Isabella?'

'Darren, what exactly…'

Her heartrate doubled as trepidation swirled through her body and the tight nugget of anxiety in her chest inflated. Whilst she had heard Darren's corporate sermons before, the fact that he was gabbling at a higher speed than usual meant she didn't have to be a contestant on Mastermind to realise he was building up to deliver bad news.

'We need to innovate to keep one step ahead of our competitors and so, moving forward, Hambleton's is ditching the sleek, clean lines of our current interior design template. Buyers don't need to be spoon-fed these arty-farty concepts. They need to know that they're not forking out for some pretentious Chelsea-type's vision and are bagging a bargain. That way it's a win-win. *I'm* not shelling out money on expensive paint and designer wallpaper and *they* know they're not being stung for useless tat that'll end up being tossed in the garbage can as soon as they get the keys. Who wants…'

Izzie could bear it no longer and a sudden surge of indignation gripped her body. She might have suffered a recent setback in her professional life, but she still believed in the positive impact good design principles brought to any building project. It was time to stand up to Darren and persuade him to consider an alternative future for Hambleton Homes. How was she to know that the director of fate had a thunderbolt tucked up her sleeve?

'Actually, Darren, I totally disagree. I've worked in interior design for over ten years now and research shows that a well-designed and presented property can increase the sale price by up to ten percent. Also, a high percentage of buyers appreciate the decorating suggestions – they might not have the time, or the vision, to make the most of a building's architectural attributes. I think…'

But Darren wasn't interested in listening to counter-arguments. He'd been repeating the words 'yes, yes, yes,' in an impatient monotone as he prepared to drop the bombshell on her already grenade-strewn world.

'So, it's nothing personal, you understand – hard decisions have to be made in business – but we've decided to dispense with your services. I'd like to take this opportunity to thank you for your invaluable contribution to…'

The force of the shock weakened Izzie's knees and she crumpled down onto the sofa. She gasped for breath as a concrete-heavy slab pressed the air from her lungs and a low buzzing sound reverberated in her ears, blocking out the finale of Darren's clearly rehearsed severance speech. However, as he continued with his diatribe of verbal misnomers, one thought did bob to the surface and a little of the old Izzie peered through the curtain of gloom.

'What about Jonti?'

Oh, God, she couldn't bear it if he lost his job too. Ever since he'd been kicked out of his parents' house in an affluent part of Cheshire, his father citing his choice of friends and unconventional lifestyle as justification, Jonti had been forced to couch-surf his way around the capital for months until he'd landed a part-time Christmas job at Harrods where he'd met Meghan. The two of them had clicked immediately and the rest was history. He'd moved into the spare room in the 1930s semi Meghan rented in Hammersmith and declared himself happier than he'd ever been, especially when Darren had offered him a few hours extra work to help Izzie whenever they needed to turn a place round quickly.

'I'll still use him on an ad hoc basis,' replied Darren rather too quickly.

Despite her own distress, Izzie experienced a surge of relief. She knew Jonti struggled to make his share of the rent. However, she wasn't completely stupid. She realised that the reason Darren was keen to retain Jonti's services had more to do with his generous sharing of his Harrods discount than his flair for interior design. Then something else occurred to her.

'Does Harry know about this?'

'I don't need my father's permission to make mundane personnel decisions!' snapped Darren, obviously offended by her question. 'Okay, must dash; things to do, people to bollock, if you get my drift. Your severance cheque's in the post. Ciao.'

An avalanche of emotions tumbled through Izzie's chest. Live cautiously was her motto; that way she would avoid getting hurt, but it was clear her strategy hadn't worked because once again life had conspired to toss another random grenade in her path.